SPRAY

HARRY EDGE

SPRAY

*Hodder
Children's
Books*

A division of Hachette Children's Books

For Conor

A Catalogue record for this book is available
from the British Library

ISBN 978 0 340 95614 4

Typeset in Baskerville by Avon DataSet Ltd,
Bidford-on-Avon, Warwickshire

Printed in the UK by CPI Bookmarque, Croydon, CR0 4TD

The paper and board used in this paperback by
Hodder Children's Books are natural recyclable products
made from wood grown in sustainable forests.
The manufacturing processes conform to the
environmental regulations of the country of origin.

Hodder Children's Books
A division of Hachette Children's Books
338 Euston Road, London NW1 3BH
An Hachette Livre UK company

CAST LIST

GAMEKEEPER – male? age? Occupation?

HAN – fifteen, female, school student

JEN – seventeen, female, school student

MAC – seventeen, male, burger bar worker

MAIKO – nineteen, female, first-year university student

JOE – eighteen, male, first-year university student

RIK – nineteen, male, university IT technician

SHELL – eighteen, female, first-year university student

ZED – nineteen, female, student nurse

WEEK ONE

SATURDAY 11.14 P.M. – MAC

Someone was after him already. The game didn't start until midnight tomorrow. There should be no immediate danger. Most likely, the assassin planned to follow Mac to his rented flat, where he would lie in wait. But that wasn't where Mac was heading.

Mac stopped suddenly. No footsteps behind him. Was he mistaken? Mac got to the tram stop and put his hood up. It wasn't raining, but the air felt muggy enough for there to be a storm. The trams only ran for another hour. He wouldn't be able to get one back.

If the target demanded it, Mac would find a hiding place. He didn't have to be back at work until two on Monday. By then, he meant to be at least two targets to the good.

The number 5 tram appeared at the far end of the street. Just then, the first drops of rain began to fall. First rain in weeks. It was warm, yet refreshing. As the tram came to a halt, a guy appeared from nowhere. Forty-something, shaved head, he paid his fare and sat three seats back from Mac. Was he the assassin? Mostly, it was teenagers and twenty-somethings who played, but there was no upper age limit. All the rules said was that you had to be over sixteen.

The light on the tram flickered on and off. A faulty bulb,

3

nothing more. Raindrops glistened on the window, backlit by sodium street lamps. When Mac got off the tram, the bald guy didn't follow. Outside, the rain had stopped almost as soon as it began. The evening had become even more humid, unseasonably sticky.

Mac examined his laminate. A scruffy guy with thick glasses had given it to him in the waiting room of a derelict bus station. For no good reason, Mac had been expecting a bloke as his first target. Instead, the guy had given him a grown woman. Jal, aged twenty-four, worked in a primary school and lived in a shared house on the east side of the city. She was pretty, if the photo was anything to go by. Mac wondered what she did on Saturday nights.

He checked his A–Z. Her house was round the next corner. It felt a little evil, arriving at a stranger's house after midnight, staking her out. What if someone called the police? The authorities knew about the game. They had tried to ban it, but there was no law against people using water pistols. To stop himself being arrested Mac only had to show his laminate. By giving their details, targets gave you permission to enter their house, as long as it was to spray, not steal. And as long as you didn't actually break in.

The house was a nondescript two storey with red paint flaking off its brick walls. There was a light on inside. The curtains were half open. Mac ducked beneath the fence at the front and waited. After a while, he used his field glasses. That was her all right: Jal, with two blokes and another girl. It looked like they were watching a movie.

Mac had confirmed his target. Now he needed a place to hide. He walked around the perimeter of the house until he found a back gate with no lock. He let himself in, hood up, hands thrust in pockets. The best thing to do would be to sneak inside the shared house, be ready to do her as soon as midnight struck tomorrow. But twenty-three hours would be a long wait, and he had just pulled a long shift. To play Spray, you had to be patient. The game was three weeks long and it hadn't started yet.

Mac would return tomorrow.

SATURDAY 11.52 P.M. – SHELL

'Where did you meet the gamekeeper?' Joe asked Shell.

'A disused garage near the mini-mart. Only I'm not sure it was a him. The . . . person was wearing this disgusting old raincoat. Yours?'

'He had a false beard and glasses when we met, really obviously fake, like he didn't care who knew. About my height.'

'Mine wasn't as tall as you. Maybe there's more than one.'

'Who cares? Want to compare targets?'

Joe gave her one of his easy, cheeky smiles. Shell and Joe had rooms on the same corridor, but this was the longest conversation they'd ever had. Shell often felt like Joe was looking down his nose at her. Which, for some reason, made Shell come over all perky and girly, a side of herself she didn't like. Yet, recently, Joe seemed to be interested in her. Earlier in the day, when they'd been testing out their water pistols at the city park, he'd followed her around until he'd given her a good soaking. Tonight, he kept flirting with her.

'I'll show you mine if you'll show me yours,' he went on.

Shell was crap at saying no. But no, she decided.

'Maybe later,' she said. Loads of people on the corridor had paid their money and tried to register for the game.

There was a limit of two hundred players. So far, only the two of them had been accepted. At some point, they might be up against each other. Secrecy, as Shell saw it, was essential.

Joe put his arm around Shell. He was very touchy-feely with other girls, but never, before, with her.

'Come on, Shell. You know you want to share.'

Before Shell could reply, Maiko knocked on her door. Shy Maiko had also applied to join the game. She seemed an unlikely assassin, but Shell suspected she had ulterior motives.

'Hey, Maiko! Did you hear yet?'

Maiko tossed back her long, dark hair and shook her head.

'Look at this.' Joe handed Maiko his card. She read it out loud:

'Prak. Works in a bank, lives on the other side of town. That sounds like a high-rise flat, Joe. Could be a tough one.'

'We've got twenty-four hours before the game begins. By Monday, I'll know his routine, get him on the way to work maybe.'

'It's weird,' Shell said, 'knowing someone out there has my room number and my email and they're coming to get me.'

'Not if somebody else gets them first,' Maiko pointed out. There was a loud *ping* from her laptop. Maiko opened it. Joe looked over her shoulder.

'Too late to back out now,' he said. 'That's your contact email from the gamekeeper.'

* * *

The Game Is On! read the subject line. Maiko opened it:

Return-Path: <gamekeeper@assassins.org.uk>
Received: from aamtain07-winn.ispmail.
nodoby.com
([81.103.221.35]) for <maiko17@hotmail.
com>;10:00:33 +0100

Thank you for your contribution. You have been registered in the game that begins at midnight tomorrow. Please read the following carefully.

You must be available to meet the gamekeeper at any time during the week before the game begins. He will email you a time and a location where you must meet him the next day. At the meeting, he will give you a manila envelope containing a laminated card that displays the following:

- a picture of your first target
- your intended target's home address
- your intended target's work address
- your intended target's name and contact details.

Keep this card with you at all times. Your mission is to find and spray (by water gun, balloon or super-soaker) the target.

You can hunt your target down however

you see fit; you can pose as a delivery person and spray them when they open the door. You may disguise yourself and soak them in the street, etc. You may not hunt them down at work (or within a block of their work), at their place of study, or on public transport (including waiting areas). Breaking and entering is also forbidden. Any infraction will result in disqualification and your target's reinstatement. You may work with other players, but there can only be one assassin, and only one winner.

Further refinements to these rules will be given to you with your target card. Rules may change or be added to. You must inform the gamekeeper of all successful soakings within four hours. Cooperation is mandatory. When you are assassinated you must surrender your target card to your assailant. If you are successful in your assassination attempt, the person you sprayed will give you their laminate. The person they were supposed to spray next becomes your new target. This continues until you have worked through all remaining players and retrieve the laminate with your name on it. At this point, you may claim your prize.

'It's so exciting,' Maiko said. 'Now all three of us are playing!'

'But only one of us can win,' Joe pointed out. 'Let's do a deal. Whoever lasts the longest, the other two will support them. Deal?'

'Deal!' the other two agreed.

They began to discuss game strategy. It was just after midnight when Maiko's email *pinged* again. The new mail was from the gamekeeper.

    You are to meet me this evening on the
    third floor of the multi-storey car park
    at 216 City Road. I will be by the pay
    machine at six-fifteen precisely. Do not
    be late or your place will be forfeit.

Her computer gave another loud *ping*. The three of them read the email highlighted on the screen. The sender was anonymous. *You are my first target* it said. *I shall take you out on Monday, at 12.01.*

SUNDAY 9.04 A.M. – RIK

Two men stood outside the hall of residence.

'Spray surveillance?' The dude talking had lank hair and a thin moustache. Age: thirty at most. 'Maybe we can help each other.'

'Sure,' Rik said. He held out his laminate. This dude wasn't his target. 'Let's see yours.'

He looked at Moustache's laminate. First name: Maiko. Law student. Nineteen years old, lived on the same corridor as Rik's target. She had no part-time job, unlike most students. Moustache wasn't allowed to break into her room or attack her in buildings where study went on, so she might be tricky to spray in the short term.

'I want to hit her at 12.01. Are you a student?'

Rik shook his head. 'I'm IT support, cover the whole campus.'

'Nice. Means you can't be sprayed here. I have a plan.'

Rik listened. He had a few plans of his own. He was going to win this game. But you had to use other players. He was happy to steal their ideas. That was how you got on.

'OK,' Moustache finished. 'All we have to do is swap cards.'

SUNDAY 11.28 A.M. – HAN

'Are you the gamekeeper?' Han asked the clean-shaven man wearing thick, dark glasses.

'No. I'm his assistant. How old are you?'

'Nearly seventeen,' Han lied. 'Do you want a birth certificate?'

'No,' the gamekeeper's assistant said, 'I'm aware that you sent in proof of age and identity, but, in person, you look very young.'

'I'm trying to,' Han said. 'That way, my targets won't notice me coming. I thought I might wear school uniform some of the time.'

'Schools break up for half term soon,' the assistant said. 'A uniform would make you conspicuous.'

'Thanks for the advice.'

He handed her the card containing the name and details of her first target. Han glanced at the contents. It wasn't who she wanted.

'Thanks,' she said to the man, whose shape and face were largely concealed by his coat and the woollen balaclava he wore.

'Good luck,' the gamekeeper's assistant said. 'I'm sorry to give you the information so late. We're short-staffed. Please wait here for two minutes before leaving.'

Han stood at the door, watching him go. He had sensed that she was too young, but didn't seem to care. Not much, anyway. Behind her, in the musty, derelict church, a rat darted between the pews. Less than a minute had passed, but it was long enough. She hated waiting. Time for Han to start her hunt.

SUNDAY 4.17 P.M. – SHELL

Shell opened the door to a plump guy with dark, curly hair. She didn't recognize him. At first, she thought he was another student. She could usually tell students and civilians apart. The guy had no-brand trainers, a plain T-shirt and baggy trousers. A screwdriver handle poked out of a front pocket. Not a student, Shell decided.

'I'm here to help with Maiko's computer,' he said.

'Tech support on a Sunday?' This had to be part of the game.

'I had a call out.'

'Can you show me some ID?'

'Course.'

He showed her a staff card that looked genuine, with photo ID. As he was putting it away, Shell glimpsed another card beneath it, a credit-card-sized laminate like the one the gamekeeper had given her.

'Can I take a closer look?'

She snatched the guy's card holder and, before he could object, had lifted the laminate high enough to read Maiko's name.

'Maiko's not in,' she told him. 'She's meeting the gamekeeper, getting her target details. So I'm afraid

14

you're a little early.' She turned round and yelled down the corridor. 'Joe!'

Joe stumbled out of his room. 'What is it?'

'You ought to meet this guy. He's Maiko's assassin.'

'Really?' Joe reached into his pocket. There was a whirring noise. The big guy seemed not to hear it, for he didn't hurry off. He had a sheepish smile on his face, like he'd been caught out but didn't mind. A real loser.

'It's only a game, right?' he said. 'Spray and be sprayed. You playing too?'

Joe nodded and reached into his pocket. Before the fake tech guy could turn around, Joe whipped out his phone and took a photo.

'Neat', the big guy said. 'Let's see.'

He leant over and looked at the picture. 'Not a bad likeness. See you later, dude.'

'I hope they're all as stupid as him,' Joe told Shell when the big guy was gone. 'One of us might have a chance of winning.'

SUNDAY 10.39 P.M. – MAC

It was warm enough to be in shirtsleeves, but Mac wore an old, grey windcheater with big pockets. He had been home for sleep, a shower, shave and something to eat. The game started in eighty minutes' time. Jal – if she was here – would be on her guard. There were no lights on in the house. Mac guessed she was away, staking out her own target. Or she and her house mates might be down the pub.

He tried the back door. Locked. He had two options. One was to sneak into the house when one or all of the residents returned from wherever they were. The other was to hide out. Jal didn't drive. He'd checked her route to work. A bus would drop her off within a block of her school, so he had to get her before she got on the bus.

He heard footsteps. One set. Was this her, coming back? No. Too heavy. Mac crouched behind the wheely bin at the back of the house. The back gate had been left open, not by him. He had a narrow view of the street. A silhouette passed. It could be, almost certainly was, the bald guy from the night before. Luckily, Baldy didn't pause, or look round, but kept walking.

OK, so Baldy must live round here. No need to be paranoid. No, take that back, there *was* a need to be

16

paranoid, but the guy hadn't spotted him. If he was playing the game, he was probably on his way to Mac's home, staking him out there. Mac had left a light on in his first-floor flat. Let Baldy watch as long as he wanted. Mac had no intention of returning tonight.

The street was quiet again. Time to find a hiding place.

SUNDAY 11.58 P.M. – SHELL

'Why aren't you out stalking your targets?' Shell asked Joe.

'I've taken a look at mine,' Joe said. 'There's no hurry. Everyone's going to be on their guard at first, running round like crazy. I plan to lull mine into a false sense of security.'

'If your assassin doesn't get you first,' Shell pointed out.

'We'll be fine if we stick together,' Joe said. 'And we already know what Maiko's looks like.'

'Really? How come?' Shell asked.

'He's there now!' Maiko said, pointing out of the window. 'He said he'd get me at 12.01 and there he is, waiting to come in!'

Something felt wrong. Nobody would be so brazen, Shell thought, no matter how stupid they were.

'Let's go and scare him off!' Joe said.

'I'll stay here with Maiko and watch,' Shell told him. Joe shot off down the corridor, yelling. Doors opened. Other students hurried out after Joe, wanting to know what the fuss was all about.

'This is exciting, isn't it?' Maiko said. 'I'm glad I let Joe persuade me to join.'

'You like Joe, don't you?' Shell said.

'Everyone likes Joe,' Maiko said, with a shrug. 'Isn't he why you joined the game?'

'No!' Shell said, as a crowd of students clattered on to the concourse outside the hall of residence. No campus security yet. The university authorities said the game was irresponsible. Bystanders could be frightened. But they weren't able to ban it.

Shell would run a mile from a real gun. But you'd have to be pretty dumb to mistake a brightly coloured plastic water pistol for a deadly weapon. People might get wet, that was the only risk. And only if they got in the way of those who chose to play. The game was a bit of fun, was how Shell saw it: a welcome release in exam season. As long as assassins didn't spray each other in lecture halls and seminar rooms, there was nothing any authority could do to stop it.

She looked at her watch. Only a few seconds before the game began. Seven. Six. Five. Four. Three. Two. One.

MONDAY 12 MIDNIGHT – RIK

Everything went according to plan.

Joe, the arrogant guy who Rik had met earlier, came charging down the stairs. There was a posse of students behind him, most of them giggling like infants in nursery. They opened the security doors as wide as they went, then charged outside. None of them noticed the dude with the moustache as he weaved his way through the crowd, ambling into the building.

'Hi, man,' Rik said, affecting a laid-back, surfer drawl. Joe gave him a smug grin. He was Rik's age, nineteen, and, unless he was a straight-A student, no better qualified. But he looked good and, in this world, good looks were all you needed to feel superior.

'You're not getting inside,' Joe told Rik. 'Maiko's protected. So you might as well go home. Leave her alone.'

'I'll leave her alone, all right,' Rik said, pointing his super-soaker. 'She's not my target. You are.'

As Rik sprayed Joe, the posse of students burst into laughter. Joe, drenched, gave Rik one terrible, furious look. Then he realized he had to take his soaking lightly or he'd appear even more stupid.

'Oh, you conned me, all right,' he muttered, shaking the

water from his curly hair. 'I suppose you want this.'

He handed Rik his target card. Rik shoved the laminate in his pocket without a glance and walked away. The watching students applauded. All the hundreds of computers Rik had fixed for kids their age and older, and nobody had ever applauded him before.

He wondered how the dude who'd helped him was getting on. What name did the moustached man go by? He should have asked.

MONDAY 12.01 A.M. – SHELL

Watching from an upstairs window, Shell wasn't sure whether to feel sorry for Joe or pleased that he'd had his comeuppance. The boy who sprayed him was clever. He'd even showed them a laminate with Maiko's details on it. Which meant that he must be in league with Maiko's assassin . . .

Shell hurried inside, up the stairs to the floor where she and Maiko had rooms. Maiko's door was ajar.

'Maiko. It's me, Shell. You've got to lock your door!'

'Too late,' said a warm, deep voice.

The guy at the door had a pencil moustache and long but thin hair.

'He knocked on the door and I opened it,' Maiko said. Her T-shirt was soaked through.

'I said I'd get you at 12.01,' the shooter said. 'Can I have your card, please?'

Maiko reached into her pocket. Shell only got the briefest glance at the picture on the card. A good-looking young guy. Moustache looked at her looking at it.

'You playing the game too?' he asked.

Shell nodded.

'Catch you later,' he said with a grin.

MONDAY 7.49 A.M. – MAC

Mac wished he had a car to sleep in. The shed he'd found was extremely uncomfortable. He'd spent the night scrunched up between a bunch of tools and an old bike. Now his legs ached. He was tired, but he was in position, crouched behind the wheely bin at the back of Jal's house. Any moment now.

A door slammed. Mac didn't know what the other people in the house did for a living, but primary school teachers had early starts, so this was liable to be her. He lifted his head above the bin lid just high enough to see out. It was Jal all right. She stopped at the front gate, and looked cautiously up and down the street. She was within range. He had to move now.

Mac tried to stand. Disaster! His leg had gone to sleep. He leant on the bin, pressing his foot against the concrete floor, trying to get some feeling back. At least Jal didn't see him. She turned left out of the front gate. The bus stop was two hundred and fifty metres away. If she ran, Mac might not reach her. Still holding on to the bin, he overbalanced. It fell on to him, bruising his thigh.

Nobody came out to investigate the noise. That was something. Mac forced himself to stand, then limped through the back gate into the street. He had worked out Plan B the night before. There were two streets that ran parallel with each other. If he ran fast enough along the back one, he could overtake her.

Mac had to work his way through the pain. He ran along the street, picking up speed, ignoring the puzzled glances of a postal worker on her rounds, a cyclist wearing a helmet. A tiny dog with big ears, perched at a window, barked loudly. As Mac passed, it scratched at the glass, as if about to leap through it. Mac turned the corner and almost ran straight into Jal, who was walking at a fast clip, her bus stop only fifty metres away.

'Watch it!' she said, in a stern, school teacher's voice.

'Sorry,' he said. Pulling open his windcheater, he revealed the pistol concealed beneath it. He gave it a couple of pumps, then sprayed her across the chest and shoulders.

Jal looked angry, angrier than Mac had seen a woman since his stepmum walked out on his dad. 'How am I going to go to school looking like this?' she asked him.

'You should have thought of that when you entered the game.'

'Touché.' She shrugged hopelessly, her make-up running, then opened her handbag. She got out the laminate containing the name of his next target. 'Good luck.'

Taking the laminate, Mac felt more alive than he had done in months. He was aware of everything going on in the world around him. It was like being in the movies, with wide screen, high definition, surround sound and even – sort of – cinematic slow motion. He was aware of Jal noticing something, reacting. What?

Mac span round. The bald guy from the tram and the night before was walking towards Mac. He had an orange super-soaker in hand. In another moment, he would be in range. Mac tensed, scoped his surroundings. There was nowhere to run.

'Excuse me,' Jal said and stepped aside. 'I don't want to get even wetter.'

Mac was stuffed. Baldy wasn't his target. Even if Mac's pistol weren't empty, he would not be allowed to shoot back. Mac had to take his punishment like a man. The only witnesses would be Jal and the cyclist wearing a helmet. The cyclist, oddly, seemed to be coming back in their direction. Baldy pointed his gun. Mac stood his ground. Braver to take a soaking than run and avoid the full force of the blast.

Mac managed to smile at his assailant. He felt like the condemned man facing the firing squad. But there was no shame in getting caught. At least he'd made one kill. The bald man's middle-aged face was serious, full of intent.

Before Baldy could press the trigger, the cyclist passed alongside him. The cyclist appeared to say something. Baldy turned to look at him, or her. The cyclist grinned and pressed a button on the bike's handlebars. A spray of water soaked the bald man. He dropped his super-soaker, glanced at Mac and shook his head.

The cyclist did a U-turn and returned to Baldy, who began to laugh in a creepy, empty way. Then he surrendered his card.

'Shouldn't you be running?' Jal said to Mac. 'The cyclist'll be after you in a moment!'

Mac took another look at his new assassin but couldn't

make out his or her face. Then he sprinted away.

Mac didn't look back, but ducked in and out of streets and alleyways, his heart pumping and head spinning, not slowing down until he was sure he couldn't have been followed.

TUESDAY 8.50 A.M. – ZED

Their living space was a metal box, little more than two metres cubed, with bunk beds on one side and a fold-up table with laptop, radio and electric kettle on the other. Their clothes were piled on the floor, except for their uniforms, which were on hangers at the end of the bunks. For washing, they had wet wipes. The portable toilet was for use only in emergencies. The overhead fluorescent light, leeching power from the street supply, flickered.

'When you suggested we move in together, this wasn't exactly what I had in mind,' Zed said.

'In the future,' Yogi replied, 'most people will live like this, in storage containers. When you get a job in a different city, your home will be forklifted on to a lorry and away you go.'

'I think most people would want windows, if only for better ventilation. Still, it keeps us safe from our stalkers.'

'How did you go on last night?' Yogi asked. He'd been asleep when she got in. He slept like a log. Full of adrenalin, it had taken hours for Zed to get off, hours listening to Yogi snore in the dark.

'I got him on the street. He'd been out on a kill himself, had a couple of drinks to celebrate success.'

'Fatal,' Yogi said. 'Come on, then, details.'

Zed gave him the details, downplaying what a thrill it had been, dwelling instead on the long hours she'd spent waiting behind a low hedge, doing occasional crunches to keep herself supple.

'How'd you go on?' she asked when she'd finished.

'We're a team, right?' Yogi said to Zed.

'Until we end up facing each other,' Zed said.

'So help me track down my target.'

'She lives in a hall of residence, doesn't she? Can't be that hard.'

'I went round there during work. Said there'd been reports of an intruder and they were all really anxious to tell the story, make it clear that this was just a laugh. Seems there were three of them in the same block playing the game. Two got blown away in the first five minutes. That just leaves my girl.'

Zed laughed. 'Five minutes! That was an expensive experience.'

'My target's a biology student, first year. When I asked to see her, everyone closed up on me. I figure she might talk to a girl . . .'

'More than half the people in the game are women,' Zed pointed out. 'They're protecting her, and they'll suspect me.'

'Not if you don't have a super-soaker on you,' Yogi said. 'Come on, you've made one kill already.'

Zed smiled, remembering the sweetness of the feeling when she'd sprayed her target. She had the laminate for her next target, but he wasn't at home, and didn't start work until this evening, when she, too, had to be at work.

'OK,' she said. 'I'll see what I can do. Is it clear?'

Yogi raised the periscope. 'Clear.'

While Yogi dressed, Zed checked her make-up, zipped up her boots, pulled on her biker jacket and unlocked the door of their immaculately concealed hide-out.

'You follow thirty paces behind, like we agreed.'

Yogi finished putting on his uniform. 'You look nothing like your photo. You're being needlessly paranoid.'

'Do you want my help or don't you? Peel off when you're sure I'm clear,' Zed said. She pushed back her long hair to reveal the gold stars that studded each of her ears. 'I'll see you tomorrow morning.'

Zed stepped outside. A hot sun beat down on the city streets. When she was sure she was clear, Zed boarded a tram, heading for the university.

TUESDAY 11.55 A.M. – SHELL

Shell was safe in the lecture hall and the corridor immediately outside. It counted as a place of work. Nevertheless, Joe and Maiko walked her across the campus. One strode in front, the other behind, ready to intercept any potential assassin. She'd thought of skipping the lecture, but that was too paranoid. Her assassin would have to be very sharp to get access to her timetable. Also, walking around with a pair of bodyguards was a thrill. This feeling – like you were on stage all the time – was one of the reasons she'd joined the game.

'I'll come for you at the end,' Joe said when they reached the lecture theatre. A brief flash of resentment crossed Maiko's face.

Exams began the week after the contest finished, so the hall was fuller than usual. It needn't mean anything that Shell didn't recognize the young woman who sat down next to her. She was in Goth gear. All black apart from gold studs and silver bangles, a leather jacket too heavy for the time of year, round John Lennon glasses. Shell tried to spot where she might have a water pistol concealed.

'Are you famous or something?' The Goth asked, as she pulled a small notebook out of her tiny bag. 'Those two looked like bodyguards.'

'Nothing like that,' Shell said.

'Or maybe your boyfriend's just very clingy. He's a hunk, though. I wouldn't mind him clinging to me.'

'He's not my boyfriend,' Shell said.

The lecturer was nowhere to be seen. To avoid talking to the Goth, Shell reached into her bag for lip balm. Mistake.

'Is that a water pistol you've got in there?' the Goth asked.

Shell gave what she hoped was an aggressive look. 'You don't belong in this lecture. So tell me straight. Are you my assassin?'

The Goth gave a wide open smile. 'I'm not. Pat me down if you like, but I'm not carrying. Here.'

She held out a target card like the one Shell carried. Her target was a bloke, not Shell.

'I'm playing the game, like you. Maybe we could team up.'

'Where's your super-soaker?'

Goth-girl shrugged. 'My target's staying away from home and doesn't start work until this evening. No point in carrying it.'

A man in a suit walked up to the podium.

'I'm afraid Professor Callan has been called away at short notice. He has promised to put the text of today's lecture on his website by this evening and he will answer any questions about it at next week's final lecture. Sorry for your wasted journey.'

'My name's Zed, by the way,' said Goth-girl. 'Fancy a coffee?'

Joe was coming to pick Shell up at five to one. She had to hang around until then.

'Sure,' she said.

TUESDAY 12.10 P.M. – MAC

Mac's new target had an unfair advantage. Mac couldn't spray him at the office, or when he was sitting in the car, because – in his job – the car counted as a place of work. Not only that, but Mac didn't have a car himself. He couldn't follow the car until the target got out of it. People in the target's job shouldn't be allowed to play the game, Mac figured. He'd watched him go into the office, now he watched him come out. His mobile sounded as he unlocked the car. The target hunched his shoulders as he answered. Was this a chance?

It was a four-door car and a three-second run. Mac risked blowing his cover and ran. He opened the rear passenger side door. The target wasn't too tall. The driver's seat was pushed a fair way forward. There was room for Mac to squash into the well between the front and back seats. He closed the door behind him and waited to see if he'd been heard. A car door opened. The passenger door.

'Get a move on!' The voice was loud. Mac had hoped for time to get his super-soaker primed. He wanted to make a kill as soon as the target got out of the car. But now he had to keep still and hope the super-soaker's reservoir was sufficiently pressurized. There wasn't much space. Mac risked repeating the problem that had nearly cost him this morning's kill. Cramp. The other car door opened.

'What did the boss say about using mobiles on duty?' Loudmouth asked. He sounded a fair bit older than the target.

The target chuckled. 'Not as much as she'd say if she knew what the call was about.'

The engine started.

'You joined it, then, the game?' Loudmouth said.

'I'm planning on making my first kill today. A student.'

'There's a special briefing notice in the patrol room. Watch out for idiots with water pistols. Members of the public might mistake them for terrorists or armed robbers.'

'Sure. You get an awful lot of armed robbers using bright-pink and green water pistols.'

Pause, then Loudmouth again.

'Where are we going? This isn't our normal route.'

'Just a brief detour. I've had a tip.'

As he drove, the target explained how the game worked, why he had to be part of it. Loudmouth wasn't impressed.

'Water pistols are wimpy things. Kids' stuff.'

'They've come on a bit since your day. Do you know how a super-soaker works?'

'Science isn't my strong point.'

'Air pressure. Each time you drive water from the large reservoir of your super-soaker into the small reservoir, it pushes up against all of the air inside. Air is compressible – you can reduce its volume by squeezing it – but water isn't. The more water you squeeze into the reservoir, the higher the pressure of the air inside. This cushion of high-pressure air pushes on all of the water in the reservoir; the water presses on the sides of the gun, trying to get outside to restore pressure balance.'

'So why doesn't it leak?'

'The only thing keeping the water in the gun is the trigger,' Mac's target explained. 'The trigger works as a lever, pressing against the plastic tube that the water goes through. The stronger the lever, the better the gun. Release the lever and the pressurized air shoots the water out.'

The car did a sudden swerve and Mac's super-soaker rammed against his left kidney, making him groan. The guys in front didn't seem to notice. Mac's gun used the CPS system – his gun had a flexible bladder that kept the water under extra pressure. It was better at retaining water pressure over long periods. At least Mac hoped it was. He hadn't had to field test it yet. Also, the CPS had a bigger range and you didn't need to keep squeezing the trigger.

'I still don't get why you're playing,' Loudmouth said from the driver's seat. 'It isn't going to make you popular at work.'

'The game makes you feel more alert, more alive, when you know that somebody's after you all the time,' Mac's target said.

'Don't you get enough of that in this job anyway?'

'No, there's too much sitting around. Here we are.'

'A café? Didn't you say places of work were out of bounds?'

'Classrooms and bedrooms are out, not coffee bars. Otherwise student players could spend their entire lives hiding on campus.'

Mac heard a rustling noise. Something landed on the

back seat. A tie. It was followed by a jacket. The target wanted to be out of uniform. The car door opened and closed. Mac had to risk getting up. He half stretched, half rolled on to the back seat. No way could he do this silently, so he spoke before he was spoken to.

'Don't panic,' he told Loudmouth. 'I'm part of the game.'

The target's partner could grab Mac, warn Yogi in time for him to run. But Mac sensed that the two men weren't buddies. Mac gave the loudmouthed partner a big grin. The partner grinned right back.

'Go get him, cowboy.'

TUESDAY 12.21 P.M. – SHELL

Zed handed Shell a coffee and they sat in the window. They were too near the door for complete comfort. At least Shell knew there was a back way out. Zed had checked for her when she went to the toilet earlier. If a threat appeared, they could bolt.

A police car pulled up outside. You didn't often see them on campus.

'You should get yourself a CPS,' Zed told Shell. 'They've got a fifty-foot range.'

That was exactly the kind of gun Shell had. Why did people always assume Shell was a wuss? She was about to explain this to Zed when she saw something that distracted her.

'Look,' she said to her companion.

The policeman – if he was a policeman – was out of the car and walking toward the café. He wore an open-necked shirt and had his right hand behind his back.

'Oh no,' Zed said, as the policeman's right hand appeared, holding a bright-yellow super-soaker. She stood up.

A bloke with scruffy blond hair was getting out of the back seat of the car.

'He's cute,' Shell said. 'Think one of them's after one of us?'

She wanted to bolt but didn't want to miss the action.

'Doesn't matter,' Zed said, as the cute guy blasted the policeman with his super-soaker. 'Now *he's* got CPS.'

Shell watched the soaked police officer reach into his pocket and hand over the laminate.

'His new target's bound to be you,' Zed said. 'Let's get out of here.'

She opened the café door.

'What about the back exit?' Shell asked.

'This way's quicker,' Zed said. 'Don't worry, he hasn't had time to reload.'

Funny, Shell thought, the way Zed seemed sure that the target was her, not Zed herself. Zed was a student too, wasn't she? Shell got a good look at the blond guy as they hurried away. Behind him, another police officer, in full uniform, got out of the car. He was laughing his head off.

WEDNESDAY 6.54 P.M. – HAN

'Where do you keep your weapons?'

'Would you like to see them?'

Han nodded enthusiastically. The assassin pulled a large tray from beneath his single bed. The tray was covered with brightly coloured plastic. He pointed at them one by one.

'This is a super-soaker with a water burst attachment. This one's got a three-way directional head for shooting round corners. This is a standard water pistol for travelling. Only a five-metre range but that's good enough for most assassinations. These are fake cigarettes with an in-built water pump. Over there's my supply of water balloons. And this is a bog-standard super-soaker.'

'Can I hold it?'

'Sure.'

Han lifted the empty gun. 'How long does the contest last?'

'In theory,' the hairdresser told Han, 'the game could go on for ever. Some people hide out and don't do any kills for the first few days, slowing everything down. That's why there's usually a rule that, if you have a week with no kills, you're out. Also, no two games are the same. In the final week, the gamekeeper always revises the rules a different way. First time, the person with most kills won. Next time, there was a last-man-standing, time-limited knock out. Ideally, it ends in a classic duel, a *Gunfight at the OK Corral* kind of thing.'

'You've read all this up, haven't you?'

'It's all on the net. I can show you where to look.'

'That'd be cool,' Han said, flicking her hair back to let him see her wide-eyed smile. 'What about the gamekeeper? Is he one person or a team?'

'As far as anyone knows, it's just one guy. He must have support. And money. The game takes place in cities all over the world. The entry fee isn't exactly high.'

'Did you meet him?'

'He handed over my first target card. The way he was dressed, big coat, sunglasses, hat, I couldn't even be sure he was a "he". What about you? Did he give you my details in person?'

'No. By email.'

'Most stuff gets done by email. I'm surprised he granted an interview to a school magazine though. This game gets written up in all of the big papers and magazines. TV too. It's a phenomenon.'

'Really? How exciting,' Han said. 'Maybe he responded to me because I asked nicely. Could you do me a favour?'

'Anything,' the hairdresser said.

'Could I have a go with the gun?'

Han was wearing her school uniform. She'd told her interviewee she was fourteen and that her dad was outside in the car (there was no car, no dad either). As the hairdresser loaded the super-soaker, she showed him a photograph.

'I don't suppose you recognize this person? They could be playing the game. It's a couple of years old.'

Her target shook his head. He handed her the water pistol.

'Will you take a picture for the magazine?'

'Sure.' He snapped her playfully pointing the super-soaker at him.

She took the camera back. 'OK if I shoot you?'

'Sure. By the time it comes out, the game will be long over.'

'I didn't mean with the camera.' Han gave him a sweet smile before using his own water pistol to soak him.

Five minutes later, when the hairdresser had got over himself, towelled off and given her his target laminate, Han tried to butter him up.

'I know you'll be following the game,' she said. 'If you come across the person from the photo, please email or text me. Here.'

She gave him the laminate with his details on as a souvenir.

'How old are you?' he asked.

'Does it matter?' she said. 'And do you think a real fourteen-year-old would turn up to interview you wearing school uniform?'

She glanced at the laminate.

'Done any research on this guy yet?'

The hairdresser shrugged. 'He lives in a very secure apartment complex and, when he's not there, he's working. Good luck. You'll need it. I can't see him falling for the interview scam.'

'Don't worry,' Han said, 'I never play the same trick twice.'

THURSDAY 12.11 A.M. – ZED

Coming off shift was the dangerous time. Zed knew she was being watched, but they weren't allowed to hit her in the building. Would her assassin spot her when she left? Not easily. She had a taxi booked. Her plan was to swing by her next target's place on the way back, check it out. She had a pistol on her, but wasn't planning to take her out tonight, not unless an opportunity presented itself.

Then she would go back to the hide-out. Would Yogi be there? He had been eliminated, so there was no reason for him not to go back to his own place. She hoped he had. His joining the game was meant to bring them closer together, but he had screwed up from the start. She'd gift-wrapped Shell for Yogi and he'd screwed up the hit by bringing his own assassin with him. You'd have thought, as a police officer, he'd be cleverer than that.

Zed changed into her street clothes, put her uniform in a shoulder bag and left by a maintenance exit. She spotted her assassin as she was getting into her taxi. He glanced in her direction, then returned his gaze to the main entrance. Not a clue.

THURSDAY 6.02 P.M. – MAC

Work was a haven, but hardly relaxing. Every time a bike passed, Mac went into a state of hyper alert, thinking this might be his assassin. The bike was his only clue. He wasn't even sure of the rider's sex. But s/he had sent him a text that morning, signed DC.

YOU'LL NEED COOLING OFF AFTER FLIPPING THOSE BURGERS, it read. SOAK YOU LATER.

DC – Dangerous Cyclist? Whoever it was would be watching him now. DC would know that the burger bar closed at midnight on week nights, might follow him on the bus the way Baldy had followed him. Mac was safe until he got on the bus. The stop was on the same block as the burger bar. But when he got off, he was a sitting target. So he had to find another way to get home, or set up a decoy. Also, he had his own target to track down. A nineteen-year-old student called Shell.

Shell had seen him. She was one of the two girls sitting in the window of the café at the university. She had hurried off with her friend, the Goth, as he was collecting the laminate from Yogi, the game-playing police officer. He could have gone after her. Mac didn't have time to reload. Even so, he could have borrowed Yogi's water pistol, and got two for the price of one. But it would have felt wrong, against the spirit of the game. Yesterday, he had been given a narrow escape. Today it was Shell's turn for the get-out-of-jail-free card.

Mac could wait outside her hall of residence all night, stalk her. But he wanted to play it clever. There must be a way of drawing her out. Mac had two hits already. If he could spray a policeman, he could surely soak a student. But, first, he had to avoid being soaked himself. He turned to Ben, his co-worker.

'Can I stay at yours tonight?'

'You're hiding out because of your stupid water pistol game?'

'You'd find it exciting if you gave it half a chance.'

'Each to his own. It sounds like tag for grown-ups to me. But you can have some floor if you want.'

'Where are you parked?' Mac asked.

'Back of the supermarket.'

That was two roads away.

'Would it be all right if you left before me, picked me up from here?'

'What am I, your chauffeur?'

'I'm being hunted,' Mac said.

'OK, OK. You finish closing up tonight and I'll give you a lift back to mine. I've got a spare blanket.'

'You're a mate.'

Outside, a bike drifted by with no lights on. Dangerous.

THURSDAY 9.24 P.M. – RIK

Rik was famous for pulling late shifts. He liked his own company and, though things still went wrong at night, there was less to do. He played games, designed software, emailed and messaged buddies. Since finishing school, most of his friends were people he'd never met. He was more comfortable that way.

This whole building was Rik's work zone. When the game was on, work was the safest place for him to be. He had even started sleeping here. Rik had a torch and a master key that let him into the bathroom. He had a sleeping roll and bag he kept in the video recorder cupboard (nobody had used videotapes for years). He might stay tonight. Or not. It depended what he saw on the screen.

On Monday, while his target was at work, Rik had erected two battery-powered videocams outside his victim's riverside flat. He'd leeched a wireless connection from her neighbours. For thirty hours, he'd had a high-res video feed of the front and back entrances. Not that there was much to see. He had only scoped her once so far. A car with shaded windows dropped her off after work on Monday. She was some kind of company director. The driver got out of the car, checked out the street, then opened the front door of the apartment for her. She rushed inside. Next morning, the driver collected her and they did the procedure in reverse. Yesterday evening, she didn't come home. She could be hiding out at a friend's, or she could be staking out her own target.

University security only did one circuit of the building after it closed, at ten. Rik had hacked into their cameras, too. Thanks to them, he was pretty sure he'd sussed who his own assassin was. She'd been hanging around the main entrance yesterday. He'd also seen her peering into the IT suite earlier, trying to make him.

The assassin probably had him down as a big, slow-moving target. But Rik had his moves. He looked at the bank of screens. No sign of his assassin. But there was a light on in his target's flat. Had he missed her going in, or was it on a timer? If it was a timer, he'd have seen it the night before. He rewound the recording until he saw a van in front of the main entry. It had been there such a short time, he'd thought it was stopped in traffic.

A worthy opponent. He wondered how many kills she'd made.

Rik fancied a night in. Some TV, a frozen pizza (no way would he risk having one delivered) and a couple of beers. If he was going to go home, it had to be now, before the building shut down. But Rik didn't want to exit until he knew where his assassin was.

There! He caught her on one of the surveillance cameras, skulking near the front entrance. She dropped out of view almost immediately, but her body language had given her away, as had the baseball cap she always wore. Rik used his mobile to order a taxi. Then he rang campus security.

'Hi, sorry to bother you guys, but I want to report a suspicious person on campus. I'm pretty sure she isn't a student . . .'

THURSDAY 10.32 P.M. – SHELL

Shell checked the game's website. The first kill reports were starting to appear. They were boastful accounts that used first names for both the targets and the assassins. Joe and Maiko were among those listed.

Some of the assassins used pseudonyms online. One, calling him or herself DC, described stalking her target ('*hard to miss, with his polished bald head*') as he stalked his, and getting him just before he made his own kill, who was now her next target. Sometimes, targets shot back, making a kill into a water fight. But it didn't matter who shot first. If you got soaked by your assassin, you were out.

Shell had yet to sight her own target. She was wary of going out unescorted, so she'd shown Joe her target card, enlisted his help. She'd thought the game would make her brave. It was like the website said: playing this game was like being in an action movie. Only Shell was the stereotypical woman victim, the damsel in distress, the one the hero tried to protect. And Joe, despite being out of the game, seemed determined to cast himself as her hero.

'OK,' he said. 'I'm off to see your target. He went out for the evening, so he might be heading home pretty soon. Will you be ready to join me if an opportunity presents itself?'

'You bet,' Shell said.

'I'll stay with you,' Maiko said.

'Thanks,' Shell said, though she didn't want Maiko around. Maiko was here because she wanted to get next to Joe. And she could have him. Until today, Shell had felt indecisive about Joe. He was convenient, but he didn't set her heart racing. As of this afternoon, she was much more interested in the guy she'd seen earlier. Another clichéd scene from an action movie: the girl who fell for her assassin. Although, in the movies, it usually happened the other way round.

'Give me a bell if he's waiting outside,' she told Joe. If the guy was there, she would go to one of the hall windows, sneak a peek.

'Sure,' Joe said, pulling the peak of his baseball cap down so that it covered his eyes.

'I wish I knew what my target looks like in the flesh,' Shell told him. They hadn't spotted her once yet. All she knew was what was on the laminate. Name: Han. Age: sixteen. Occupation: student. Shell, Joe and Maiko had both hung around the exits to her college at the end of the day. None of them had spotted her. Han supposedly lived in a flat, on her own. But she was never in.

'Maybe you should come with me to her place now,' Joe suggested. 'Try to get her to come to the door.'

'She'd never fall for it,' Maiko said.

'And what if my assassin's waiting outside?' Shell asked.

'I'll tell you what,' Maiko said. 'Let's do an early morning attack. I've had an idea how we can make it work. Up for that?'

'Sure,' Joe said. 'But I'll go and check her out now anyway.'

They agreed to meet at six-thirty. When they were gone, Shell switched off her lights, then went to the window. A guy who had been standing under a tree abruptly turned and walked away. Was that her assassin? It was too dark to tell.

FRIDAY 00.15 A.M. – MAC

Mac pulled down the shutter and waited for Ben's car. It was lucky, he thought, that the burger bar closed at midnight. Some places stayed open until one, even two. He'd chosen this job because it was the sort of place where they didn't check your papers too closely. He'd lied about having experience. Luckily, you didn't need any experience to flip burgers.

No sign of the cyclist. It was another hot night, unusually so for the time of year, but very windy with it. Not a night for staking out a hall of residence. By now, Mac thought, DC would be outside his flat. But s/he wouldn't have any idea where Ben lived.

According to the rules of the game, it was OK to spend one night away from your home. You must inform your assassin (via the gamekeeper) if you went outside the game area. In theory, if you were gone for two consecutive nights, you could be eliminated. The rule was unlikely to be enforced because you could be on a stake out.

The gamekeeper communicated solely by email. Mac would check his at Ben's before going to sleep.

A car pulled up in front of him. Not Ben's. The door flew open.

'Quick!' said a guy in the back seat. 'They're on to you. Get in!'

'What are you on about?' Mac asked.

'Look behind you!'

Mac looked. Four people were running down the street. One appeared to be carrying a baseball bat.

'They want the keys. Come on. We're on your side. Get in!'

Mac's heart pounded. He was in danger, he knew, but where was the threat? The guys in the car or the guys on foot? Where was Ben? It was too late. The team with the baseball bat were upon him.

'It's your funeral,' the guy in the back seat said, slamming the door. As the car drove off, the four guys reached Mac. They launched into a stream of obscenities that concluded:

'Give us the keys and get out of here!'

Mac stood his ground. He was pretty sure he was being set up. These guys were working with the guys in the car. And if this was part of the game, these four weren't allowed to use violence. But what if they weren't?

'This is your last warning!'

Should one of them hit him, Mac would run. Otherwise, he had to stay put. Where was Ben?

The guys surrounded him. They were all a little older and taller than Mac. Now he saw that the thing one of them – the leader, he assumed – held was not a baseball bat. It was a super-soaker, extended length, special edition, blue and silver.

'I'd run away if I were you, squirt,' the leader said, 'or you'll get very wet.'

'Do your worst,' Mac said. 'I'm outside my place of work. Soaking me here doesn't count.'

At last, he heard the bronchitic engine of Ben's old car. Some instinct made him glance behind him. There, silhouetted in the car's headlights, was a cyclist. She or he waved. Mac waved back. By unspoken agreement, Mac's four pursuers began to laugh. The one holding the super-soaker slapped Mac on the back.

'Worth a try, eh?'

FRIDAY 00.19 A.M. – SHELL

There was a gentle knock on Shell's door. Shell felt her heart thump. She wasn't expecting anyone. Maiko had gone to bed. What if the curly-haired guy had persuaded someone to buzz him in?

'Who is it?'

'Joe.'

She opened the door for him. 'Any luck?'

He sat on the edge of her single bed. Shell took the chair.

'I hung around that seedy flat for an hour. No lights. No noise. Either she's out stalking her own target, or she's lying low.'

'Thanks for looking, anyway,' Shell said. He deserved a hug. Or something. But she didn't want Joe to think she was coming on to him.

'We'll get her. Even if she's cheating by living somewhere else. Maybe it's time for you to get in touch with your target, taunt her. You have her email and mobile number?'

'I don't want to speak to her,' Shell said, sorry to sound so wimpy. 'I can't make myself sound threatening.'

'Why don't we compose an email together?' Joe suggested.

'I dunno.' Shell looked at her watch. Twenty past twelve.

They were getting up at six-thirty. But she wouldn't doze off easily tonight. She opened her laptop and sat on the bed next to Joe.

'What shall we say?' she asked, as he leant closer to her.

'How about: *you can run, but you can't hide.*'

FRIDAY 7.21 A.M. – HAN

GAMEKEEPER COMMUNIQUE NUMBER 1

Return-Path: <gamekeeper@assassins.org.uk>
Received: from aamtain07-winn.ispmail.nodoby
.com ([81.103.981.35]) for <addresslist
concealed>;76.00.36 +0800

Four days gone and already a third of
you are also gone. Most of you receiving
this are serious players with one or
even two kills under your belt. As for
the rest – you don't deserve to be in the
game if you can't make a kill by the end
of tomorrow. If you don't make a kill by
then, your target will be reassigned,
and you're out. Oh, and those of you who
gave fake details in order to join in,
you're out too. What do you think this
is, a virtual game?

Han read the email twice. All week, she'd been dreading the
email throwing her out. But this wasn't it. The gamekeeper

55

was bluffing, she decided. He hadn't busted her or she would have heard directly. Han didn't live where she was meant to live. There were bound to be other players in her situation. They wanted to be in the game but didn't live in the city, so got a fake address. Most would stay with friends, but Han didn't have any friends in the city, so she was squatting in an empty flat. She could have raised the money to rent, but that would have left traces, which she didn't want to do.

The squat had no electricity. That was OK. Han wasn't there much. She could recharge her laptop and mobile when she went home. Half term began today. Mum thought Han was off on a school camp until Tuesday. The cash fee Mum gave her for this had come in useful, kitting Han out with water pistols and other incidental expenses. If she survived into the game's final week, things would get a lot trickier. But Han's aim wasn't to win.

Han was leeching a wi-fi connection from a flat across the road. Her only other email was a threat, evidently from her assassin. Threats were meaningless, Han thought, then changed her mind. They were a way of raising the temperature. She emailed her target.

```
Don't think that working sixteen-hour
days will keep you safe. You'll be too
tired to see me coming.
```

Then she closed her laptop down to save battery power.

FRIDAY 7.30 A.M. – MAC

It was hot, even this early in the morning. Mac felt conspicuous in his oversized denim jacket, beneath which was concealed his super-soaker. Ben had spent the night on his sofa. This morning, while Ben slept, Mac borrowed his car to get to the student's place, arriving just in time to see her head off with two of her mates.

Mac followed them from a distance, like they did on the TV, and nearly lost them a couple of times. Stupid thing was, the place they were heading for was two streets away from his flat. He didn't see them park, but saw the two mates on the street, talking to a postman. Money changed hands and the bloke put on the top half of the post guy's uniform. Then he headed round the corner.

Shell would already be lying in wait, hidden in a doorway, her water pistol in her hand. Mac tried to work out his tactics. He didn't know which flat Shell's target lived in. He could drive up to Shell when she broke cover. But would it work? He'd have to find her, stop, wind down the window and get out his pistol before spraying her. She'd have every chance to clock him and run away.

Mac should have persuaded Ben to get up, come with him. Might as well let Shell spray her victim, then catch her

57

unawares. That way he'd get the new target laminate from her. As far as Mac could tell, there was no advantage to be gained by spraying more targets than your competitors. Let Shell do the work and have her moment of glory.

FRIDAY 7.51 A.M. – HAN

Someone knocked on the front door. Her first visitor. Ten to one it was her assassin, making good on the threat of the night before. Han looked through the door's fish-eye spy hole. A young bloke in post worker's uniform. Should she ignore him? Han didn't want to give the impression that she was never home. But why would she get post? Nobody outside the game knew that she lived here. And the guy looked very young for a postman. She called out.

'I'm not dressed. What is it?'

'Letter that needs to be signed for.'

'Put it under the door. I'll push it back.'

'Sorry, I have to see you sign it.'

'Tough luck. I'm in hiding. You've heard about this water pistol game that's going on all across the city?'

'I've heard about it, but I'm not in it, I swear.' He held up his hands, which contained only a single letter. 'Look, no water pistol. You're safe.'

He'd reacted too quickly, Han decided, too smoothly.

'Sorry,' she said. 'I can't trust anyone, and I'm not expecting any mail. Why don't you push one of those I'm-sorry-you-were-out forms under the door and I'll collect the letter from the post office when I'm out of the game?'

'This is a guaranteed next-day-delivery letter,' the guy said, sounding a little too anxious. 'It has to be in your hands today.'

'Then whoever sent it shouldn't have insisted on it being signed for, should they?' Han argued, more convinced than ever that this guy was her assassin. 'Look, I'm going back to bed. Forget it.'

She went to the window. The postman waited a while to see if she changed her mind. Then he went round the corner without leaving any kind of form for her to fill in. The mirror she'd positioned on the window frame showed him walking away. He didn't visit any other flats. Han was about to go back to bed when she saw a girl with long hair step out of a doorway. She was carrying a super-soaker. Now Han knew what her assassin looked like.

FRIDAY 7.54 A.M. – MAC

Mac pulled up a few feet from the jacketless postman, who was waiting with the other girl, facing away from Mac. They were too preoccupied to turn round. Any moment now, Mac thought. He leant down, grabbed his pistol and pumped it a couple of times to ensure maximum pressure. He looked in the rear-view mirror. Shell and her friend hadn't returned. They were probably having a laugh, collecting the card off the victim. Mac shuffled from the driver's seat to the passenger seat, ready to get out. It would only take him a moment to be out of the car, soaking Shell from head to toe.

A green car pulled up behind him. It was the car he'd been following, only now the guy who'd been driving was in the passenger seat. Shell was in the driver's seat. Damn! The guy got out, shaking his head. Shell stared straight ahead. Mac cursed. He hadn't expected her to be so clever. To get her in the car now would be too difficult. Shell would see him get out and lock the door before he got to her. Better to lie in wait at her hall of residence. Could Mac shuffle back into the driver's seat and get away without being noticed? He checked the rear-view mirror. The postman put his gear back on while the guy got back into the car. Mac would duck, wait for them to get out of sight, then follow. With luck, he'd get her in the car park.

A horn sounded. Despite himself, Mac looked around. The red car was alongside him, winding its window down. Shell gave him a big grin and a little wave. The guy – her boyfriend, presumably – pointed a super-soaker out of the window. He sprayed the side of Ben's car. Shell pounded the horn again and drove off, at speed. Humiliation.

No point in following her. Mac drove round the corner. Had Shell just made a kill? If not, he might be in a position to check out the home of his next-but-one victim. These were old buildings, a couple of them derelict, all of them divided into flats. Any one of them could belong to Shell's target. Slowly, carefully, Mac drove back to his own flat, circling the streets around before parking outside, keeping a wary eye out for his own assassin, with or without her bike. But the only person he recognized this warm morning was the postman who had helped Shell earlier, going about his rounds.

FRIDAY 11.02 A.M. – RIK

Rik showered at work then, thinking he was safe, took the service that ran from the university to the city centre every fifteen minutes. He knew as soon as he got on to the bus that he'd made a mistake. He was preoccupied with his target. She was hardly ever home and seemed to spend the time when she wasn't working stalking her own target. The videocam he'd trained on her flat was a waste of time. She never took risks with her exits or entrances. The key must be to get her during work hours, but out of the office. Which meant he had to do her today or wait until Monday.

He'd taken a stupid risk. His assassin came from nowhere and got on the bus just before it left. She had jettisoned the baseball cap, but he still recognized her at once. She wasn't allowed to spray him on public transport, but as soon as Rik got off, he would be in trouble. Either Rik had to stay on the bus until it reached the end of the line, or he would risk being sprayed.

He thought she'd take a seat by the door, for an easy exit. Instead, she came and sat next to him, then started talking like they were old buddies.

'That was a good move last night, getting security to kick me off campus.'

She was snub-nosed, kind of pretty. Small but built. Girls like this didn't normally talk to Rik, not unless he was fixing their computer.

'So I take it you aren't a student?' Rik mumbled.

'We're all students of this vast cosmos, aren't we?'

'Have you got any kills yet?' Rik asked, keeping his voice low.

'You'll be my first. You?'

'One.'

'Well done.' She held out her hand. 'I'm Jen.'

Her hand was surprisingly slender and cool. 'My friends call me Rik.'

'I've been watching you for four days,' Jen said. 'And I like what I've seen. I'd like to get to know you when all this is over. Would it be OK if I called you?'

'You're just trying to soften me up for the kill,' Rik's words stumbled out.

'What if I am? I still fancy you.'

Rik felt himself blush. He'd never had a girl tell him she fancied him before. 'Uh, yeah. You can call me,' he said.

'Thanks.' There was a long, awkward pause before she spoke again. 'How are you going to play this?'

'I haven't decided yet,' Rik said.

'This bus goes in an endless circle. Did you know that? We could stay on it all day.'

'Then I guess we'll get to know each other pretty well.'

Jen grinned. She had a nice grin. 'What kind of ticket did you buy?'

'A return to the city.'

She held out hers. An all-day pass. 'Your ticket runs out

as soon as we leave the central zone. I can get you thrown off the bus. Looks like I've got you trapped, big man!'

FRIDAY 11.23 A.M. – ZED

'Let me help you,' Yogi said as Zed raised the periscope of their storage container. The street looked clear.

'You're not in the game any more,' Zed pointed out. 'You could lose your job. I don't want to be responsible for you being sacked.'

'Let me worry about that.'

'But I do worry. Anyway, it's cheating. You're allowed to have people help you, but a police officer? That's crossing a line.'

'How about if I don't help you get your target, but I watch your back? If I'd had somebody watching my back I'd still be in the game.'

'That makes sense, I guess . . .' Zed didn't like to argue too strongly. Yogi was still her boyfriend. He'd stayed in the hideout with her last night, but wouldn't tonight, because she was going back to the nurse's quarters, where she was supposed to live, in order to fulfil the game's residency rule. There was no point in playing a game if you didn't stick to the rules.

That said, all rules could do with a little bending.

'There is one other favour you could do me,' Zed said. 'You'll need to be in uniform.'

'Anything,' Yogi told her. 'My shift doesn't start until one. Until then, I'm yours.'

FRIDAY 11.30 A.M. – RIK

Jen was so cool that Rik was almost tempted to let her spray him. They talked about his job, movies, the shop where she worked and where they bought their water pistols.

'Mind if I get up?' he asked when the bus reached the business district.

'Getting off?' Jen asked, with a cheeky twinkle in her voice.

'I'm going to change my ticket for an all-day pass.'

'Good move. I'll be right behind you.'

A trail of people were getting off the bus. Rik waited until they'd gone before he went to the front. He had to push his wide body around the people getting on.

'Scuse me. Coming through. Scuse me.'

Jen followed in his slipstream. She had an open bag at her side. A super-soaker or water balloon was bound to be within easy reach. A woman with a pushchair got on and Rik saw his chance.

'Let us help you with that,' he said as she folded up the chair and sat her son by the hold. Rik took the folded chair from her. He lifted the contraption up as though about to place it in the hold.

'Thank you. That's very kind,' said the young mother.

'Not really,' Rik said, looking behind him. The last person was getting on the bus. He only had a moment. Instead of putting the chair down, he thrust it at Jen.

'All yours,' he said, and let go of it.

Despite herself, Jen caught the chair. Rik backed off the bus.

'Don't let her off,' he called to the driver. 'She's trying to steal that pushchair!'

The driver gave Rik a confused look. Then, as Rik was hoping, he closed the door. Rik strode into the busy street. By the time Jen got the driver to open the door again, Rik was out of sight. His heart leapt. Whether Jen fancied him or not, it was good to know he had a worthy opponent.

FRIDAY 12.38 P.M. – ZED

Yogi met Zed on the corner by the hotel. He had questioned the hotel manager, as she'd asked, pretending her target was a crime witness.

'His shift starts at one, so he should be here soon. Great timing.'

Zed thanked him. 'You get off. I can manage from here.'

'If you say so. But first, there's someone I need to talk to. Don't look round yet.'

Yogi charged off. Zed gave it a moment, then she turned to see what was going on. Yogi was in conversation with a slender guy who had a thin moustache and long hair. Despite the dry summer heat, he wore a trench coat. No wonder Yogi was suspicious.

How had Zed's assassin spotted her? He must be good. She had covered her tracks so carefully. Zed decided there was only one thing for it. She strode off in the opposite direction, past the hotel entrance. She wanted it to look like she was running away.

When she was out of sight, she doubled back on herself. An alley ran along the rear side of the hotel to the service entrance. That was the way her target, a porter at the hotel, would come to work.

A hot breeze from a ventilation shaft ran down the alley, adding to the sultry summer heat. Zed rang Yogi on his mobile.

'Did you get rid of him?'

'Sure. I watched him walk away. We could find an excuse to arrest him if you want. Concealed weapon.'

'It's a game. The whole city knows about the game.'

'Yeah, but everybody knows city cops are stupid. Love you.'

'Love you too,' Zed said, though she had her doubts these days. 'Can you keep an eye out until just before one?'

'That's why I'm here. We're only round the corner from the station. I can be a few minutes late for my shift.'

Zed already had a place to hide in, a big metal bin. The bin was emptied daily so shouldn't be too filthy. Zed opened the bin, took a quick glance at the disgusting debris at its base, then clambered inside. Oh well. She was wearing old clothes. Being smelly was part of the price of playing the game.

Zed checked her watch. The more conscientious workers would be arriving for their shifts soon. She didn't close the bin completely, but jammed the lid open with her pocket periscope. Then she pumped her super-soaker, priming it for action.

FRIDAY 12.51 P.M. – RIK

The sleek black building soared so high, Rik couldn't see its apex from the city street. His target worked on the twenty-third floor. He had never seen her in person, but should recognize her from a distance. Only trouble was, he had yet to observe her leaving the office at lunch. He might have to hang around until the end of the day. If he did that, there was a big risk Jen would find and spray him.

One good thing about the target's office: it had no parking garage, only a covered drop-off bay at the front. So, wherever she parked, his target would have to leave the building by foot. Probably.

Rik re-examined the target laminate. Age thirty, investment banker, single, specs. Whenever he'd seen her, she wore jeans, even for her high-flying job. She was cool, a high flyer. In no other circumstances would Rik get her mobile number. He hoped his story was good enough to fool her.

FRIDAY 12.55 P.M. – ZED

Zed's mobile vibrated against her thigh. She checked the message from Yogi. Her target was about to turn down the alley. She looked through the periscope. There were three men coming. All wore the porters' grey uniform. At this distance, Zed couldn't tell which of them was her target. She could spray them all, but that was against the spirit of the game and, anyway, Yogi could be wrong. These could be decoys. She had to wait for them to get closer.

Her heart pounded against her chest. Any moment now. The periscope wasn't as effective as she'd hoped. The images were too small for her to make a definite identification. At a guess, hers was the man in the middle. He had his shoulders hunched and his head down, like he was trying not to be noticed. Yes, that had to be him. He was three paces away.

Zed withdrew the periscope and punched the metal bin lid open. The guys on either side of her target looked shocked. As well they might. A tall woman with huge hair, a military jacket and filthy jeans was pointing a giant-size red super-soaker at them. She grinned. They broke to either side of her target. Zed squeezed the trigger.

The target ducked, then hit the ground. He tried to roll

over. But it was too late. He was already wet and getting wetter. The target put his hands up.

'Stop, stop! You win!'

Zed hauled herself out of the metal bin, bits of greasy paper sticking to her bum. She landed heavily on the ground, dusted herself down, and walked over to her very wet target. His fellow porters were grinning. Zed held out her hand. He shook it.

'Every day this week I got somebody to check that bin. Today, these two told me I was being paranoid. You were lucky.'

'You make your own luck,' Zed said. 'Can I have your target laminate?'

'Of course.'

The porter reached into his pocket for a wallet. From the other end of the alley came a call. Yogi.

'Hey, Zed. Gotta go to work. You be careful out there!'

'I will!' Zed called, taking the laminate.

She was about to read her new target information when there was a tap on her shoulder.

'We meet again,' said the cool-looking guy with the moustache.

From his trench coat, the long-haired guy pulled out the biggest super-soaker she'd ever seen. Its spray was so wide, so dense, that within a second she was soaked. She turned and tried to run away. This only made her back even wetter than her front.

'Had enough?' asked the moustached man.

Zed nodded. She handed him the laminate, which he wiped dry. 'You got me good.'

73

'At least,' the slim stranger said, 'you have had the honour of being beaten by the game's eventual victor, the legendary Zorro.'

FRIDAY 12.59 P.M. – RIK

Rik called his target's office and established that she was on her lunch break. Then he double-checked the location. The office building only had one exit. At one, floods of people left through the double doors, but not her, not unless she was a master of disguise. If she were going out for her lunch, she'd have gone by now. It was time to activate Plan B.

The police station was two minutes' walk from the office. In the foyer, Rik brushed past a very wet woman. She was with an officer in uniform. The woman was either a spray player or she had just taken a swim in the pool by the ornamental fountain. The uniformed officer was distracted. He seemed to be apologizing to her.

'I'll get you dried off.'

'You said you could start your shift a few minutes late. I thought you were looking out for me!'

'I'm sorry, I'm sorry.'

'I had two kills. It was going so well!'

'Will you get her out of here?' The desk sergeant called. 'She's dripping all over the floor. It's a health hazard!'

'There's a bathroom through here,' the officer told the woman, flustered. He turned to Rik. 'Can you hold this thing open, mate?'

'Sure.'

The officer swiped his card and the security barrier lifted. Rik had an idea. He'd meant to call his target on the mobile phone, but this game was all about seizing your opportunities. He walked confidently through the barrier, following the wet woman. There were several open-plan desks ahead to his right, but Rik didn't want anybody to hear his call. This was lunch time, so most offices should be empty. However, he didn't know the police's shift system. He'd never been in trouble with the law and didn't want to start now. The secret was to move fast, and with confidence. A door to his right was ajar. He prepared an excuse and pushed it open. Empty. Yes!

He closed the door and picked up the phone. Most places, you dialled '9' for an outside line. Here, it didn't work. He tried '0' instead. Result.

The phone was answered on the fifth ring. Rik gave his target's full name and the name of the officer whose office he'd 'borrowed', Inspector White. He did his best to sound like a senior cop.

'I'm afraid there's been a complaint about you.'

'Who from?' Her voice was clipped, calm.

'I'm not at liberty to say, but it involves an allegation of assault.'

'That's ridiculous. This must be some kind of a joke.'

'I'm afraid not, ma'am. We have to take allegations of this sort very seriously, even if we suspect that there may be ulterior motives.'

'Ulterior motives? This is about the game, isn't it?'

'What game would that be?' Rik tried to sound ignorant.

'How do I know that you're a police officer?'

'You can call me back on this extension if you want, ma'am, but you must call me back at once. Otherwise I'm afraid I'll have to come and interview you in your office.'

'This is nonsense. I'm calling the police station now.'

She hung up. Rik waited for the phone to ring. And waited. Had she failed to call? Or was the police switchboard busy? He had heard stories of people making emergency calls and being kept on hold for ages. This was hardly an emergency, but it *was* the police. Come on!

The office door opened.

'Who the hell are you?'

Rik nearly panicked. He was used to working for university bosses, few of whom were comfortable with their own authority. If one of them found a stocky, long-haired nineteen-year-old sitting behind their computer, they assumed he had a right to be there. But this guy sounded like a bully. Rik gave the only answer he knew.

'Inspector White? I'm Tech support. They told me there was a problem with this computer but it seems OK to me.'

The inspector cursed. 'Thing keeps freezing up. Annoying as anything.'

'Is there a particular application you're using when this happens?' Rik asked, knowing that at any moment the phone would ring and give him away. He had to get rid of this policeman pronto, or clear off himself.

'Word processing's the only thing that's always on.'

'You've probably got some kind of software conflict. There's a program I can run. Can you spare the computer for a few minutes?'

'How many are a few?'

'Fifteen, tops.'

'Very well. I'll come back in fifteen. Thank you.'

'No problem. It's what they pay me for,' Rik said.

The phone still didn't ring. Best to fix the computer if he could, so Rik ran a quick diagnostic check. There was a common conflict. The officer was using the wrong version of a mapping program. Rik downloaded the right one and replaced it. Two minutes' work. He picked up the phone to call his target again. Engaged. What should he do now? Maybe it was time to get out of here.

The phone rang. Rik answered at once.

'White.'

The target apologized. 'They kept me on hold. Look, I realize you're genuine but I guarantee that this is a wind up.'

'I see,' Rik said. 'But we have to take all complaints seriously. I take it you don't want me to come to your office to question you?'

'That would be seriously embarrassing.'

'Then perhaps you can get here safely. I need a brief interview.'

'I guess ... I can call a taxi to our entrance. He or she's not allowed to attack me there. Can I count on you to cover me at the entrance to the police station? I'm sorry, I know it sounds silly. But this is a game that you have to take very seriously.'

'Very well,' Rik said. 'But please try and get here within ten minutes. I have a number of other people to see.'

'I'm on my way.'

'Call me on this number when you're about to arrive and

I can make sure there are no people with water pistols waiting at the door.'

Was getting her to call him again ridiculously risky? Jen would be impressed. Rik sat at the desk and, to distract himself, goofed around on the Internet. He read the accounts of recent kills on the game's website. Some people were up to three already. One player was described as a 'legend' who had won two previous tournaments. He called himself 'Zorro'. According to the website, Zorro had long hair and a thin moustache. Rik wondered if he was the bloke who he had helped get into the hall of residence earlier in the week.

He was clearing the browser cache when two things happened. The phone rang and the door opened. Rik answered the phone.

'My taxi's just pulling up. Do I ask for you in Reception?'

'No need,' Rik said. 'I'll meet you there.' He cut off the call but kept talking. 'Yes, I thought that must be the conflict. Before I reactivate the system I want to be sure that there are no more potential problems.' He paused. 'I see. OK, thanks.'

Now he needed to get out as quickly as possible. He stood up and spoke to Inspector White, who didn't look too happy about Rik using his phone.

'All sorted. To avoid this sort of thing happening in future, please check with us before you download any new software. I know it's inconvenient, but, in the long run, it will save you time and keep the department working within legal guidelines.'

The officer gave Rik a shifty look. Good guess. Ninety per cent of computer users had some kind of dodgy software, including police. Now the guy couldn't wait to get rid of Rik.

'That's most helpful, thank you. Now if you don't mind, I . . .'

'I'm already late myself,' Rik said. 'I'm out of here.'

He hurried back out of the office, hoping he would be able to intercept his target with the water pistol concealed in his baggy jeans.

FRIDAY 1.26 P.M. – ZED

Zed left the women's rest room at the central police station. She had dried herself off the best she could, leaving her with ratty hair and a soiled left leg where she had brushed the inside of the bin. Yogi was waiting by the main entrance, looking anxious. He was meant to be out on patrol, not looking after his humiliated girlfriend.

'You got two kills,' he reassured her. 'That's two more than I did.'

'Thanks for reminding me I'm going out with a loser!'

A woman charged through the door. Smart, with expensive glasses, probably a lawyer. And she sported a tell-tale bulge in her large Gucci bag. Seeing Zed clock her water pistol, the woman's gaze moved to the fluorescent handle poking out of Zed's shoulder bag. The woman began to back into the door.

'It's cool,' Zed called. 'I just got eliminated from the game.'

The smart woman forced a smile. She turned to the desk sergeant. 'The officer said he'd meet me out front.'

The sergeant gave a pretty good approximation of a growl.

'Which officer would that be? Presumably one who knows

you're trying to enter a police station while carrying a concealed weapon.'

'Um . . .' The woman wasn't going to drop the officer in it by giving away his name. The desk sergeant started to go off on one.

'Because I am pretty fed up with constant security alerts caused by a childish game that involves people pretending to be terrorists while wasting litres and litres of tap water, of which, in case you hadn't noticed, there is a shortage. And this officer here is already thirty minutes late for his shift because he's been helping his very wet girlfriend get dry, which she could just as easily have done at home. But if you'd care to tell me which officer has promised to protect you, I'll buzz him – and I presume it is a him because my officers only tend to make a fool of themselves over women offenders – and get him to come and collect you. But only after I've given him a bollocking!'

The desk sergeant paused for breath and, as he did, noticed someone behind Zed. 'You, did you want something?'

Zed, Yogi and the water-game woman turned to see a large guy with long hair and the world's baggiest jeans. He had a zen smile and his hands in his back pockets. His voice was high, a little nervous.

'Sorry to interrupt, but is this lady here to see Inspector White?'

'I am, and I have less than half an hour of my lunch break left. Where is the inspector?'

'He's waiting on the other side of that door, ma'am. I don't know how you missed him.'

'Oh.'

'If you'd just go ahead of me.'

'Very well, but I thought we were meeting in—'

The big guy interrupted her. 'You can't take that water pistol inside a police station, ma'am, it counts as a concealed weapon. That is a water pistol in your handbag, isn't it?'

'Yes, but—'

'Just go through that door, please.'

Yogi and the desk sergeant exchanged bemused glances. As he followed the woman through the door, the fat guy began to pull a long, thin super-soaker from the back pocket of his jeans.

A moment later, they all heard an angry scream.

'Why couldn't you be more like him?' Zed asked Yogi.

SATURDAY 9.14 P.M. – SHELL

The email from the gamekeeper was very clear. Either Shell got a kill by midnight tonight, or she was out of the game. The gamekeeper, unlike her assassin, had her mobile number. She could get a call eliminating her at any moment. And her target wasn't home. Shell hadn't even set eyes on her yet. The only proof of Han's existence was that Joe had spoken to her through a door.

Han, whoever she was, didn't have a job, and didn't appear to study where she was meant to study. But she lived where she was meant to live. So Shell couldn't report her for cheating. Shell had one chance. She'd managed to talk herself into a flat across the road from Han. From here, she was within range to soak her target at a moment's notice. If she came home. And if Shell's own assassin didn't get her first.

SATURDAY 10.43 P.M. – MAC

'You want fries with that?' Mac recognized the guy he was serving but he wasn't sure where from.

'Yeah, a regular portion. So you haven't got her yet?'

'I beg your pardon?' Mac took the guy's money.

'My girl Shell. You're stalking her, right? I'm Joe.'

Mac remembered him now. 'Are you in the game?'

'Got taken out.'

'Bad luck,' Mac said, though this guy looked the lucky type – more likely he was out because of bad play. 'How did you find me?'

'Spotted the car down the road. Bit of a giveaway.'

Mac hadn't thought of that when he borrowed Ben's car. Stupid of him. What was this guy leading up to? Mac made conversation.

'Thought I had Shell the other day. You guys were too fast for me.'

'Might as well give up now,' Joe said. 'Her protection is too good.'

'Hard to protect someone all the time,' Mac pointed out. 'How many hits does she have?'

'None of your business,' Joe said, taking his change. He hesitated. 'You seem like a smart guy. What are you doing working in a place like this?'

'Lots of smart people work in places like this,' Mac pointed out.

Joe gave a brief nod, then left. Mac was good at reading people. Joe's visit had told him two things. First, Shell wasn't Joe's girlfriend, not yet, anyway. And second, Shell hadn't made her first hit yet. So the chances were she was still stalking the flat he'd nearly caught her at yesterday morning. Question was, could he get over there without alerting his own assassin, the anonymous cyclist? He turned to Ben.

'Can you give me a lift tonight when we finish our shift?'

SATURDAY 11.09 P.M. – HAN

In the dark, expensive city centre bar, the guy with the shaved head and the heavy gold jewellery was showing off to anyone who'd listen.

'My assassin will be waiting for me outside my flat. But I've got no intention of going home tonight. I've got two kills already. This is my night off. Only question is, who will I be spending it with?'

The woman he was chatting up gave a fake smile then turned back to her mate. Certain she'd found her target, Han took the free seat to his right. It was a risk. This was an over twenty-ones place. Even in this low light, and with the amount of make-up she had on, Han couldn't pass for eighteen, never mind twenty-one, not close up. Whereas her target was almost thirty. She didn't know how to chat up a bloke like this. She didn't know how to chat up a bloke full stop. She got out the photo she always carried with her.

'Excuse me. While you've been playing this water pistol game, you haven't come across this guy, have you?'

Han's target glanced at the picture, then he glanced at her, to make sure that she wasn't carrying. He took in her tight dress and tiny purse, decided that he was safe. 'He's a player?'

'I think so. He's an old friend I need to track down.'

'Need? Sounds urgent. Tell you what, give me your number, I'll call you if I see him.'

'That's nice of you, thanks. But I can never remember my number. Give me yours and I'll call you.'

He did, and she typed it into her phone.

'Maybe I can buy you a drink,' he said.

'A lager would be great.' Han didn't want the barman looking at her and she needed to get to a tap, so she made her excuses.

'I just need to visit the little girls' room. Back in a mo'.'

In the toilets the water pressure was really low. It took Han a couple of minutes to fill the balloon she had hidden in her purse. When she'd got it to bursting point, she tucked the bloated balloon behind her back and returned to the bar. Her target was paying for the drinks. He had his back to her, with his phone out, ready to take her number. Hannah stopped at the far end of the long bar. She couldn't resist using her free hand to text him: GOT YOU AT LAST.

'You were going to call me,' he reminded her, as she sat down and took a sip of her drink. His phone vibrated. He smiled again, then checked the message. Han smashed the water balloon all over his shiny head and trendy suit. Her victim swore.

'What the hell do you think you're doing?' the barman asked. 'I'll have the police on to you.'

'You've ruined my phone!' the target protested.

'That'll teach you to come on to a girl half your age,' Han said, then turned to the barman. 'And I hope you have fun explaining to the police what you were doing serving a sixteen-year-old.'

It annoyed her, having to add a year to her age, but she didn't want her target to know she was too young to be in the game. The soaked slaphead handed over his laminate without further protest.

Han hurried out of the bar before the situation turned nasty. She could have pumped her victim for info about her next target, but she wouldn't trust anything he told her. Time to return to her stuffy squat. She would email the gamekeeper with news of her triumph.

SATURDAY 11.59 P.M. – SHELL

The flat's occupants were away for the weekend but had lent Shell a key. She could get into the stairwell, but not the flat itself. There was a peephole through which she could see her target's flat and whoever came to the door. She'd been looking through it for two hours and needed a wee.

Just before midnight, there was a light knock on the door. Shell let her visitor in.

'You're safe,' Joe assured Shell. 'Mac's shift doesn't finish until one on a Saturday, so he can't get away for another hour. And he's paranoid about his own assassin.'

'It's nice of you to come,' Shell said. 'I thought you were going out with Maiko.'

'A bunch of us went to the movies, but I made an early escape. I put you first,' Joe said.

Shell didn't know how to interpret that. She knew how much Maiko liked Joe but not how much Joe liked Maiko. Or her. If Shell didn't encourage him soon, it might be too late. She was flattered that Joe was interested, all of a sudden, but that didn't mean she had to be interested back. Best to leave things and see how they developed.

'There's a way you can help me,' Shell told Joe.

'Anything.'

'I think she'll come back in a taxi and only stop if the road is clear. Then she'll use the taxi for cover while she nips into the flat before I can get across the road, spray her.'

'So what do you want me to do?' Joe asked.

'Delay her. It means waiting in the street where you can't be seen, then blocking her door when she gets back.'

'She'll assume I'm her assassin.'

'Exactly. While she gets out of your way, she won't be looking for me.'

SUNDAY 12.21 A.M. – MAC

'No cyclists in sight,' Ben said.

His car was in front of the burger bar with the engine running.

'Let's go.'

'Hey, what's going on?' A male voice.

Mac twisted round, worried that the speaker was his assassin. But he recognized this guy, a regular.

'You're meant to be open until one on Friday and Saturdays!'

'I know, I know, but these are special circumstances.'

'Can't I just—'

'Sorry,' Mac pulled down the metal shutter. 'You can buy a microwave burger at the petrol station down the road.'

'I don't have a microwave.'

'They'll heat it up for you there.'

'I don't want to walk to the petrol station. Do you know how hot it is out here?'

'So get an ice cream instead,' Mac said, padlocking the shutter. 'Gotta go.'

As they drove off, Mac passed a posse of people on the corner. One of the silhouettes looked familiar. It was DC. He still couldn't work out his assassin's gender. Mac was trapped by his shifts. DC was bound to catch him sooner or later. How was anybody supposed to win this game? That was it, Mac decided. He was always going to quit the burger bar when the game was over. But his game would be over much quicker if he didn't quit now.

SUNDAY 12.31 A.M. – HAN

Han didn't go straight back to the squat. The club where she'd sprayed her victim was on the far side of town. Han used her travel pass to check out her next target. He wasn't home, which was probably for the best. Han only had one spare balloon on her and balloons were only good for close work. She would collect her super-soaker and return the next day.

Han caught a tram and got off two stops from her house, where there was a taxi rank. The tram conductor gave her a funny look when she flashed her child's tram pass – not many under-sixteens around after midnight. The taxi driver gave her an even funnier look when she told her how short a distance she wanted to travel.

'You can walk there in five minutes.'

'I know, but I don't feel safe. There are people after me. I want you to park right in front of the flat and wait until I'm safely inside. Can you do that for me?'

The woman gave her a sympathetic look. 'I'll do it, no charge, but take a bit of advice from me. You're never going to be safe in an area like this. How old are you? No more than seventeen, I'd say. Haven't you got some family you can go back to?'

'I have. I'm going home soon,' Han said.

But not, she hoped, too soon.

SUNDAY 12.34 A.M. – JOE

Joe waited outside Han's flat. He tensed up when he heard a car coming. Not many car owners on this street. Could be her. Joe was here because he wanted to be with Shell. It turned him on that she was in the game when he wasn't. It turned him on that she played it so cool. Maiko was beautiful but she kept making it clear that she had a crush on Joe. For some reason, this was an enormous turn off. Whereas Shell never flirted with him, rarely even smiled, no matter how much he helped her out.

A taxi rounded the corner. Han, the target, sat in the front passenger seat. This was going to be easy, if they played it right. As the car stopped, a phone rang. Nearby, but not his. Joe didn't dare step out of the doorway to find out where the noise was coming from. At least Han couldn't hear it, not while she was in the taxi.

The phone stopped after the third ring. The taxi door opened. Han got out. Seeing her for the first time, Joe was impressed: black cocktail dress – very elegant, not your typical assassin. The taxi door stayed open. Han didn't appear to have paid yet. But she was almost at the door of her flat. Timing was everything. Joe made his move. He charged out of his shaded doorway, almost smashing into Han.

'Who the . . . ?' Had it been Shell standing in the shadows, she would have sprayed Han by now. Where was Shell?

'What is this?' The taxi driver was getting out, a mobile phone in her hand. 'I'm calling the police, I warn you.'

'No need!' both Joe and Han said at the same time. Han, close-up, was surprisingly young. She reminded Joe of his little sister, who was fourteen. But you had to be sixteen to play this game. The girl looked Joe up and down.

'Where is it then? Your water pistol?'

'I'm not in the game,' Joe said. He pointed over her shoulder. 'But she is!'

Shell was holding her super-soaker, but did not point it. The taxi driver, seeing Shell with the gun, seemed to get the message.

'You lot are playing that stupid water pistol game. I should have known. Biggest water shortage in the country's history and a bunch of kids decide it's a great time to waste water by spraying each other on the streets!'

She got back into her car and drove off, the passenger door bouncing shut as she rounded the corner at the end of the street. Han was fumbling with her key to get into the flat.

'Spray her!' Joe shouted. 'Spray her!'

Shell shook her head, and the girl was gone, inside the house.

'I set her up for you!' Joe said. 'What are you playing at?'

Before Shell could answer, another car turned the corner. 'Quick!' Joe told Shell. 'Get back inside! That guy's your assassin!'

'He can have me,' Shell said.

'What's got into you?' Joe asked her. 'Why have you given up?'

The car pulled up alongside Shell. Mac, the guy from the burger bar, stepped out of it. Shell put her hands up. Mac looked surprised, like he couldn't believe his luck, but he pressed the trigger. He had his pistol set to 'intense stream'. A thick torrent of warm water belted Shell. Mac seemed determined to empty his chamber. His spray moved up and down Shell's body, giving her a full soaking, from head to toe. Shell smiled like a little girl who was having fun. Was she flirting with Mac? Joe felt a hot flush of jealousy.

'That feels great,' she said. 'It's been so hot all day.'

Mac smiled. 'Can I have your laminate please?'

'I'm afraid not,' Shell said.

The smile faded from the assassin's face. Shell explained.

'The gamekeeper rang me five minutes ago. Since I haven't made any kills in my first six days, I'm eliminated from the game. So your soaking me doesn't count.'

Joe grinned. Shell wasn't such a victim, after all. The guy driving Mac's car called out to him.

'Did I hear right? This was a wasted journey. We risked closing early for nothing?'

'Afraid so,' Mac told him.

'I've had enough of this. I'm going home. You coming?'

'I just need to talk to this girl for a minute.'

'I'm going now. If you want a lift home, get in!'

'I can't go home,' Mac said. 'Too risky.'

'Suit yourself.' The guy in the car drove off.

Mac shook his head.

'Looks like you're stuck with us,' Shell told Mac.

'I could think of worse people to be stuck with.'

'Me too,' Shell said.

'So who's my target now?' Mac asked Shell.

'I expect you'll get an email about it tomorrow.'

'Let's hope I can find somewhere safe to read it.'

'Do you want somewhere to hide tonight?' Shell asked him. 'It's the weekend, so there are lots of empty rooms in our hall.'

'Really? That'd be great. Where is it?'

'Joe will give you a lift. Won't you, Joe?'

'Eh, yeah, sure,' Joe said, though he didn't like the idea one little bit. Shell and Mac got into the back of Joe's car. So much for tonight being his lucky night.

SUNDAY 11.34 A.M. – RIK

The doorbell rang as Rik was getting out of the shower. Nobody visited him on a Sunday. Most of his friends slept even later than he did. Suspecting a trap, Rik nearly didn't answer it, but the second ring was more insistent. He pressed the intercom button.

'Who is it?'

'It's Jen, from the bus the other day.'

'That's nice,' Rik called back. 'You'll understand why I can't let you in.'

'I'm safe,' Jen said. 'I've been assassinated.'

Rik hesitated. 'How do I know you're not bluffing?'

'Have a look at the game website. I was sprayed last night. I thought I'd come and tell you what your new assassin looks like.'

'Thanks,' Rik said. 'But let me take a look at the site first.'

He pulled on some jeans and a sweatshirt while his laptop booted up. No time to dry himself properly. Was this girl interested in him? What could she see in a fat slob who mended computers for a living? More likely this was a trap. But no, there it was on the site, a boastful account of how this dude, who called himself Drizzabone, had 'offed' Jen by hiding in her parents' garden and catching her on her way back from a failed attempt at her target.

Rik opened the door to Jen. She was wearing exactly the same clothes combination as him.

'Either you're really good at hacking web pages or you're being straight with me,' Rik told her.

'I thought I ought to warn you what your assassin looks like.'

'Nice of you, but he's already had thirty-eight hours to spray me.' Rik felt bad about moaning. He liked this girl. But he found it hard to believe that she liked him.

'I could hardly spray you yesterday. You worked a double shift.'

'How do you know that?'

'I persuaded one of the tech assistants in Audio Visual that you were my boyfriend.'

'What?'

'I did this little-girl act like I was worried that you were cheating on me because you worked all these odd hours. So she told me I could check your schedule with her any time and what a nice guy you were and she was sure you wouldn't mess me around.'

'Clever,' Rik replied.

'Want to know what your new assassin looks like?'

'Good idea.'

Jen got out her phone and transferred two photos to his laptop.

'Anyone you've seen around?' Jen asked.

Rik shook his head. The guy had studs in his eyebrows and a barcode tattooed on the side of his neck. That was so last century.

'Maybe you could use a little help,' Jen suggested. 'And it so happens that I suddenly have time on my hands.'

WEEK TWO

SECOND MONDAY 6.14 A.M. – HAN

Han was pretty sure she'd had a narrow escape. Who was the guy who jumped out from a doorway and why had his girlfriend not sprayed her? It made no sense, but it was a lesson. She would be more careful next time she returned to the squat.

Han had to stay in the game if she was to find Chris. She'd shown her fourth target the photo yesterday, directly after spraying him, but he didn't recognize him. All he'd said was: are you sure you're old enough to be in this game? But he didn't complain. Who wanted to embarrass themselves by revealing they'd been taken out by a fifteen-year-old girl?

Han checked the game's website. More than half the players had now been eliminated from the game. She was one of only three people on four kills: the others were Drizzabone and The Invisible Man. The leader, with five kills, was someone who called himself Zorro.

Time to go out and track her fifth target. According to the game's website, the target had only made one kill, on the game's very first day. She called herself Dangerous Cyclist. DC for short. Han had questioned yesterday's target – a dentist who she'd tracked down on the golf course – about her. The target said he'd only glimpsed DC twice. She wore androgynous clothes and a helmet that hid her face. She had a team of helpers, who stuck with her much of the time.

'You've got no chance,' the target told her as he handed over his laminate. 'You might as well give up now. I did.'

SECOND MONDAY 9 A.M.
– GAMEKEEPER

The gamekeeper had a whiteboard where he kept a list of
assassins and their targets. Now that more than half the
players had been eliminated, he updated it constantly,
shuffling names around until he could see the state of play.
The first time he ran the game, he'd tried to keep it in
alphabetical order, but that meant rewriting everything,
several times a day, and it was still easy to make mistakes. So
he put the changed targets wherever there was a gap on the
board. Soon, there would be more gaps than there were
players left.

Han – Dangerous Cyclist
Badmonkey – Famefan
Dangerous Cyclist – Mac
The Invisible Man – Obelisk
Deniro – The Cartoonist
Rik – Deniro
Senile – Suburbgirl
Zorro – Factoid
Mac – The Invisible Man

The gamekeeper wrote the name 'Lol', then checked his watch for the second time since arriving. He and his assistant had four new laminates to give out today. It was easier to make new laminates than it was to collect the old ones from players he had eliminated. The losers tended to resent being thrown out. Some of their complaints were valid. The gamekeeper did keep some of the game's rules vague, and he didn't publicize the 'no kills in six days and you're out' rule before play started. Each game was different. He had to ensure that the game worked its way to a thrilling solution within the three-week time slot. That meant adapting to circumstances.

This time round, a lot of players were being cagey, more concerned about not being sprayed than they were about spraying their targets. Maybe it had something to do with the heatwave, the water shortage. But it got hotter and drier every year in most countries where the game was played. And the game got harder.

This game meant more to the gamekeeper than other games because it was in the city of his birth. He had been away a long time, and it had changed a great deal, but it was still home. One day, he would give up the game and settle down somewhere, maybe go back to university or start a business. This could be the place. And one day he would like the world to know he'd been part of this game, long before the rip offs that were bound to come: the dumbed-down movie version, the reality TV series, the things the media did to make the wonderful commonplace, the weird the same, the whole world over.

'You're late,' he snapped at the youth who joined him in the bus terminal.

'Sorry, rush-hour traffic.'

'I have other people to see. Here's your new laminate.'

'Thanks.' The guy, who called himself Mac, stared at the gamekeeper. They hadn't met before. The gamekeeper's assistant had handed out most of the laminates, but had had to return to his own country for work. That meant the gamekeeper was on his own, which got a little boring and lonely at times.

'You're younger than I thought,' Mac said.

The two men were the same height, not far apart in age or looks. The gamekeeper should have disguised himself more. Today, he'd put on glasses with the plain lenses, but hadn't bothered with the hat or the raincoat. They would have made him too conspicuous in this heat, so he'd gone for a green hoody and jeans.

'Everyone tries to look older than they are,' the gamekeeper replied. 'Until they start trying to look younger than they are. In my experience, very few people are happy in their own skins. Are you?'

'I don't know what happiness means,' Mac replied. He glanced at the laminate. 'This "Invisible Man", how many kills has he got?'

'I can't give out information that helps a particular player,' the gamekeeper told him. 'You'd better check the website. But be wary: not everything people claim on there is true.'

'Thanks for the warning.' Mac leant forward and shook the gamekeeper's hand. Surprisingly few people did this. Mac's handshake, like the gamekeeper's, was firm.

'Good luck,' the gamekeeper said in parting, surprising himself, for he never had favourites.

SECOND MONDAY 1.38 P.M. – RIK

Rik sat in his office, waiting for Jen to ring. He was good at waiting. Here, he was safe from Drizzabone. He'd always been cautious. Had to be. Big men made easy targets. He'd always been large, heavy. Heavy people were more likely to fall through thin ice.

Rik didn't like being a wimp. By playing this game he hoped to turn one of his weaknesses – his hesitation – into a strength. And it was a thrill. He'd never felt better than he did after spraying the posh banker at the police station. Telling Jen about it, watching her eyes light up as he described how he set her up, that was a thrill too.

Rik had never had a girlfriend, never really considered romance a possibility. But when he saw that glow in Jen's eyes, anything seemed possible. He mustn't build his hopes up, though. He had every reason not to trust her.

This afternoon, Jen was out helping him to track his next victim. Rik was using the university surveillance cameras, on the look out for Drizzabone. It was handy Jen had taken that photo of his assassin, as there was nothing about him on the web. The game's site held only the stark information that he was in joint second place. Rik, with only two hits to his name, would be way down in the rank order. But it was where you finished that counted.

Rik's next target was the trickiest yet. Deniro drove a taxi for a living, so her place of work was mobile, as well as invulnerable. He didn't know how many kills she had, but he knew she must be good, to make it through to the second week. He would have to be better.

It was a pity Rik didn't drive, that would make things easier. He'd had lessons, but most cars were a really tight squeeze for him. He'd tried cycling, and quite enjoyed it, but people took the micky when he wobbled past. These days, he used less public forms of exercise.

He was still trying to work up a plan when his mobile rang.

'She's got a husband who works at home,' Jen told Rik. 'She stopped by for lunch but he brought it out to the car, sat there and ate it with her. They were looking round all the time. It's not going to be easy to get her. She'll need to get out to use a toilet sometime, but we've no way to follow her twenty-four/seven.'

'Never mind,' Rik said. 'I've just had an idea. How are your acting skills?'

SECOND MONDAY 6.11 P.M.
– HAN

DC was tall, with a strong jaw and high cheekbones. She lived in a block of flats overlooking the river. The river didn't offer much of a view. Over the last few weeks it had become a mucky trickle. The discarded junk of generations of city dwellers poked up from the river bed. There were still crayfish and other hardy creatures for the anglers to catch, but only the suicidal would risk eating them.

The key, Han decided, was to find out where DC kept her bike. DC's flat was on the eighth floor, so she was unlikely to keep it there. And if she did, she would have to carry it down in a lift, making her vulnerable. The bike made her hard to hunt down on the road, but before she was on the road it became a weakness. Han had to find it.

The flats were newish, expensive. DC claimed to work as a cycle courier. In which case, she either had very rich parents or was couriering goods that were both illegal and very expensive.

Han walked along the riverbank. This gave her a good view of the rear of the block, where DC lived, but no access to it. Han had to walk on to a footbridge, climb up and then go back along a road. As she did, a cyclist hurtled past her on the bike path. Was that DC? Han had no way of knowing.

Should Han spray this cyclist at random? It made a kind of sense, but could get her into trouble. The bike helmet concealed the cyclist's head. A loose body suit in red fabric made it hard to tell if Han had just been passed by a man, or a flat-chested woman. Even so, Han had an instinct that this was her target.

The apartment block, like many built this century, had a series of secure lockers for residents to keep their bikes in. The lockers had no labels, only numbers and swipe card readers. You couldn't see inside them. Han decided that she needed somewhere to hide. But first, she was going to take a look at DC's flat.

In the apartment block's airy courtyard, Han stood by the elevator. She got out her mobile and pretended to make a phone call, waiting until a resident came by. He used his swipe card to summon the lift. Han followed him into the elevator when it arrived.

'Eight, please.'

On the eighth floor she walked down a long, airless corridor until she found DC's number, 845. She knocked on the door, just to be sure nobody was there. Han could have rung the buzzer downstairs, but DC, if she was in, would have sussed her. Whereas now, if Han pretended to be a neighbour, there was a chance that her target would come to the door. A tiny chance. You weren't allowed to break in and spray someone, but if a target was foolish enough to open their door, spraying them was fine.

No reply. There was nothing to stop Han breaking in and snooping round to get intel on her target. Except the law, of course, but Han had a fake ID and wasn't bothered about the law. She was only bothered about whether she could use her credit card and pocket knife to deal with the lock on DC's door.

She couldn't. The lock was strong and sophisticated. The door fitted too closely. Han's only chance of spraying DC inside this block was to chat up one of the neighbours, see if she could hide in a flat as her last assassin had tried to do. But that approach hadn't worked when the girl student tried it on Han and it was unlikely to work on DC. Moreover, even if she got in, Han would be stuck inside a flat, with no sure way of telling when her target was coming. Whereas what she really wanted to do was to locate Chris.

You didn't need a swipe card to go down the elevator or get out of the building, so Han made a hasty retreat.

In the elevator, Han thought about her real target. There was a chance that Chris had not registered for the game. But she doubted it. Han remembered how, when they first read about the Spray game, Chris became obsessed. He would haunt websites, play endless videos, join fan forums. Han had done the same since he left, hoping to find him online. However, aside from a couple of grainy snaps with fuzzy images that could have been anyone, she'd found no sign.

Chris would have registered, she was sure of that. Only death would stop him. And if he was dead, she would have heard. Chris might have been knocked out of the game already, but Han doubted it. Chris was smart enough to get to the final rounds. And so was she.

SECOND MONDAY 7.45 P.M.
– RIK

The heat had yet to drain from the day. Rik waited in the shadows of a recessed doorway. The store it opened into had closed a few minutes before. The street beyond was nearly deserted. Rik had an escape plan ready for if Drizzabone came looking for him, but he didn't want to use it.

Rik worked in this store a couple of days a month, on his uni days off, giving computer advice to wealthy shoppers. The manager had offered him full-time work. It paid better than the university, but Rik wasn't interested. Not challenging enough.

If Drizzabone sprayed Rik here, it wouldn't count as a kill. Technically, this was Rik's place of work. He had listed it on his game application. But that felt like bending the rules. He'd rather not put the situation to the test. He had, therefore, taken extra care not to be followed when he got on the bus.

Deniro's taxi pulled up just before eight, as Rik and Jen had planned. He could imagine the dialogue inside the car.

'Wait there a minute, please,' Jen said. 'I want to be sure the store is still open. They keep changing the evenings they open late.'

Jen got out of the car and seemed to stumble. The taxi's windows were shaded. Rik couldn't see the driver's reaction, but she must have seen it, she must be concerned. After a moment, Deniro wound down the window. Good. But Rik wasn't allowed to spray her in her car, because it was a place of work.

'Are you OK?' The taxi driver called.

'No. I hurt my . . .' Jen put a hand to her head.

'Get back in the car. The store's closed. I'll drive you to a doctor.'

'Thanks. I . . .' Jen took the hand away from her head, having burst the fake-blood balloon she'd pressed against it. As the dark-red stuff gushed down her face, Jen fell. She hit the ground so hard that Rik was momentarily concerned for her. Oh, she was a good actress all right. It was going to be great, having her on his team.

Deniro, looking anxious, hurried out of the car over to Jen.

'I'm going to call an ambulance. Speak to me. How the hell did you manage to do this?'

Jen blinked one eye open. 'I didn't,' she said. 'Sorry.'

Rik let loose with his super-soaker. He unleashed a strong spray from his primed Power Burst Pistol, deluging the taxi driver. The overspill washed the fake blood from Jen's face.

'Enough! Enough already!' Deniro told them. 'You got me. I was on the lookout for that woman in the smart suit. She kept trying to flag me down then find an excuse to get me out of the car. So you must have already sprayed her?'

'Certainly did,' Rik said.

Deniro nodded appreciatively. 'How many kills are you on?'

'You're my third. You?'

'Four. Wait a minute.'

She got back into the car and came back out with a cleverly designed water pistol the length of a car seat, with a long, narrow shaft and a fat, stubby handpiece that acted as a reservoir.

'It only holds a quarter of a litre, but it has a great range. You're going to need every advantage you have if you're going to get this guy.' She handed Rik her laminate. 'He's a tough one.'

Rik read the laminate, half hoping it would be the guy he'd met on his first kill, the guy who he'd since worked out called himself Zorro. But this guy was much older, older than Rik's parents.

'The Cartoonist,' Rik said. 'He looks vaguely familiar.'

'You think you know him?' Jen asked.

Rik thought for a moment, then shook his head.

'People often give really bad photos on purpose,' Deniro told them. 'I've never seen this guy up close. He lives in a high-security block.'

'He has to go out sometime,' Jen said.

'Only at night and only, as far as I can tell, when he's on an assassination job. Look at the game website. He's on four kills too.'

'I'll get him,' Rik said confidently. 'Thanks for being a sport.'

'Don't thank me. Thank your girlfriend. She's a good con artist.'

Rik grinned at his target. 'Any chance of a ride home?'

'As long as you've got the money to pay.'

Rik had enough. He had a return bus ticket, but he figured the taxi fare would be worth it for the extra information he'd pick up about The Cartoonist. Anyway, he couldn't take Jen on public transport with her clothes still smeared by fake blood. People might think he'd done it to her.

SECOND TUESDAY 11.23 A.M. – GAMEKEEPER

They were falling like flies. Since the gamekeeper eliminated all players without a hit, the remaining players had been busy. He had accepted two hundred entrants. Three-quarters of them had already been sprayed. At this rate, the game might finish early. On the website, defeated players had opened a book on who would win. Zorro was the favourite, closely followed by The Invisible Man. But the website was full of misinformation. The third favourite was a player who claimed to have four hits, but – only the gamekeeper knew – didn't actually exist. Or if he existed, was using a different name.

He had seen it in other cities. There was a flurry of publicity and people tried to crash the game. Suddenly there were people with super-soakers in plain view. It only added to the excitement. Without their laminates, the wannabes couldn't participate, not even if they got lucky and sprayed a proper player. But they added to the general confusion, which only made the game more interesting.

He turned on the TV. The main story was a nationwide drought. Reservoirs were at their lowest levels since records began. The government were talking about bringing in

119

water rationing. Supplies would be cut off for large parts of the day.

'The hosepipe and car-washing ban is no longer enough,' the Environment Minister said. 'I am asking people not to take baths and to limit their showers to a maximum of four minutes. But if we don't get rain by the weekend, we will have to take more drastic measures.'

The chirpy presenter came back on. 'Before the weather report, there are some people who don't seem bothered by the water shortage – players of the world-famous Water War game that came to the city last week. Police say that numerous incidents involving water pistols have been reported, but there have been no injuries.' She grinned at the cameras. 'That is, unless you count injured feelings. Take a look at this CCTV footage, shot in the doorway of the city's central police station yesterday lunch time.'

The gamekeeper smiled as a smartly dressed woman was soaked by a fat guy in overalls. Who was that big youth? He checked the wallchart, which had photo IDs by each name. The guy called himself Rik. Three kills. His next target was hard, but all targets were hard at this stage. The gamekeeper took a look at who his assassin was. A nobody. Maybe Rik had a chance. Anyone with the chutzpah to do a hit in a police station had to be taken seriously.

SECOND TUESDAY 8.17 P.M.
– SHELL

'He really is invisible,' Shell told Mac. 'Either that or he doesn't exist.'

'According to his profile, he's thirty and he lectures at your university. How can he be invisible?'

'Half the staff here seem to be somewhere else half the time. When I went to his office, there was a sign up saying that he's away all semester on "research leave".'

'But if he's playing the game, he must be around. Joe and Maiko are both willing to help stake out his home address.'

'But what if he's not there?' Mac asked, adding, 'I'm never at the place where I'm meant to live.'

'Joe said he'd drive you round there later if you want to check your mail, get some stuff.'

Mac gave her a funny look.

'What?!' Shell said.

'Nothing. I'm grateful for his help.'

'But?'

'But it's not me he really wants to help.'

'You think he wants to keeps tabs on what I do with you?'

Mac shrugged. Shell didn't know what to do about Joe. It was true, she had a bit of a crush on Mac and Joe must have picked up on this. But Mac only treated her like a mate. Give it time and he might notice how her eyes lit up when he came into a room. Maybe he'd noticed already, but wasn't interested. Or he might be convinced he was too young for her. He wasn't.

There was a tap on Shell's door and Joe pushed it open.

'I got a result!' he announced. 'Look what I found!'

He held out an A4 notice.

'Where did you get that?' Shell asked.

'I went to the Sociology department where The Invisible Man works. This was on the noticeboard. That's his real name, right?'

'Oh yes,' Mac said.

'Sounds like an interesting seminar,' Shell said. 'Pity it's three days away.'

'And remember, we can't get him at work,' Mac said.

'Yes, but you can get him on the way to or from work,' Joe pointed out. 'At least now we know that he's around.'

'So you're good for the surveillance tomorrow? Mac asked.

'I'll do the first shift, from daylight. Maiko will relieve me at half seven, then Shell at nine.'

'Great.'

'Can I have the notice?' Shell asked.

Joe handed it to her. She pinned the small poster to her noticeboard. The title of the seminar was:

Water Wars.

How water pistol games have sublimated the violent urges of a generation and become THE game of the twenty-first century.

122

SECOND WEDNESDAY 6.53 A.M.
– RIK

'It's good of you to come this early,' Rik told Jen.

'No worries. I know you have to be at work at one. This morning could be our best chance for a while. Have you brought it?'

'Oh yeah.'

Rik got out the laptop and showed her what to do.

'Make it as obvious as you can. If we can draw him out . . .'

'Surely he'll think that I'm in the game and will spray him.'

'You're right,' Rik said.

'Unless I dress like this.'

Not sparing Rik's blushes, Jen pulled off her sweatshirt and tracksuit bottoms. Beneath them, she wore a skimpy orange bikini.

'No way I could conceal a super-soaker in this, right?'

'Eh, right . . .' Rik said, hoping that his face hadn't turned as red as it felt to him.

Jen grinned and put her clothes back on. 'By the time we get there, it'll be so hot outside that half the city will be wearing swimsuits. Maybe we can hit the pool after we've sprayed him. Have you got some trunks?'

'Eh, somewhere.'

'Dig 'em out, big boy. We've got time.'

While Rik got out his swimming trunks and a towel, Jen went to check the street outside. She came back to tell him that it was clear and their taxi was waiting. Her smile was so wide, Rik felt like he could conquer the world. But the pair of them still had to find a way into The Cartoonist's building.

SECOND WEDNESDAY 10.11 A.M. – SHELL

The young couple waited outside The Invisible Man's house.

'Maiko said she'd be here,' Shell told Mac.

'We are a few minutes late.'

'I'll call Joe on my mobile,' Shell offered. She did. It went straight to answering service. She tried Maiko instead. It rang several times, then cut off. Call refused. Shell figured that she and Joe must have finally got it together. Well, good for them.

'I think it's just you and me,' she said to him.

'There's no need for you to stick around,' he told her. 'If you want to get back and join your mates in hall, I'll understand.'

'I'll help you out until you get eliminated,' Shell said. 'That's if you want me to . . . quick, kiss me!'

'What?'

Shell flung herself at him, letting her long hair cover her face. She wrapped her body around his so that, to anyone passing by, the main impression would be of a very pretty, affectionate girl sucking the face off a hapless boy. After thirty seconds, Shell took her lips away and looked over Mac's shoulder once more.

'It's all right, she's gone.'

'DC?'

'Thin, wearing a red top, white helmet, green racing bike.'

'Sounds like DC.'

'I don't think she was expecting to find you here or she'd have slowed down. It looked more like she was out on a general recce.'

'DC must be getting desperate,' Mac said. 'He or she's been after me for nine days. If she doesn't spray me soon, she's bound to be thrown out of the game.'

'I don't know why you say "he or she",' Shell said. 'If that was DC, she's definitely a woman.'

Mac didn't reply. His face was flushed, Shell saw. Maybe kissing him had been a mistake.

'I'm sorry if I embarrassed you,' she told him. 'Thing is, I've seen people do that in the movies and it always seems to work.'

'I know what you mean,' Mac said. 'Playing this game, I often feel like I'm in a movie. That's part of the thrill, isn't it?'

He showed no sign of wanting to kiss her again.

SECOND WEDNESDAY 11.30 A.M.

Jen got into The Cartoonist's apartment block easily, by pretending to be the daughter of a tenant who was hard of hearing. An oldish lady on the way out let her in. Rik tried a similar ruse. He pretended to be a computer technician who was there to help a deaf man reboot his computer. But his story didn't work on anyone coming out.

'Can't you email or text him that you're waiting downstairs?'

'Sorry, this building has a very strict security code.'

'Can I see your ID? This says you work at the university. What are you doing making house calls?'

'What deaf person? I'm on the building's social committee and I don't recall anybody with hearing problems on any of the floors.'

'Um, I guess he's shy about it,' Rik told the last speaker. 'Why don't I email him?' He retreated to a park bench nearby. At least this would give him a good view if Drizzabone came after him.

Jen phoned. She was setting up Rik's laptop in an alcove near The Cartoonist's flat.

'There are loads of surveillance cameras around, but I seem to be in a dead spot.'

'Think you could come down and pretend to be going out, then let me in?'

'Not really. They have a camera on the door. It'd look really suspicious. You'll find a way. Be patient. I've found The Cartoonist's wi-fi signal, but I can't work out his password. Any ideas?'

'Hang on.' Rik had a second laptop, borrowed from work. He found an unsecured wireless network which he tapped into. Then he spoke to Jen again. 'I want you to let me into your laptop by remote access.'

Once she did this, Rik could see her computer, through which he could locate The Cartoonist's network. Cracking the wi-fi password shouldn't be hard. The night before, Rik had researched The Cartoonist's life and work over the net. In real life, it turned out, the guy was quite famous. That was why Rik thought he looked familiar when he saw the laminate. Rik knew the names of his parents, his ex-wife, his pet fish and his one son. He tried them all. None worked.

Rik kept at it. Maybe the guy actually did what everyone was meant to do but hardly anybody did. He was using numbers as well as letters in his password. Rik tried a thousand combinations, two thousand, three thousand, ten thousand . . . good thing he had a program to generate the passwords for him, or he'd be here all day.

'Everything all right?'

The guy standing by him wore overalls that looked too hot for the scorching day. He had brown hair and film star features.

'Eh, yeah, sure,' Rik said. A second sense sounded as the guy sat down next to him. This guy was a game player, no doubt about it. But no way was he Drizzabone, not unless he was a master of disguise and had just had his tattoo surgically removed.

'You want some help getting into that building?'

The grey light on the top right of Rik's Macbook turned dark black. The last password had made a connection. He could use his target's broadband. Now Rik had to find The Cartoonist's computer password. Once he had that, he would be able to find out everything about him. And he wanted The Cartoonist to know that he knew.

'I do,' he said. 'Can you help me?'

'Depends,' the newcomer said. 'Are you playing the Spray game?'

'Sure am.'

'I'll help you get in if you help me get my next target.'

'Are they in the building too?' Rik asked.

'Not at the moment, but they will be.'

'You've got a deal. I'm Rik.'

'People call me Lol.'

SECOND WEDNESDAY 11.47 A.M. – SHELL

When Shell got back to hall, Joe and Maiko were already there. They weren't sitting too close together, yet Shell could tell at once that things had changed between them. Joe looked like he was trying to suppress a grin, while Maiko was glowing. Romance was in the air.

'Where were you earlier?' Shell snapped.

Each of their expressions became sheepish.

'I think it's time to pull back a bit from helping Mac,' Joe said.

'We *were* there,' Maiko said. 'But—'

Joe rapidly explained, talking over Maiko. That morning, Maiko had turned up on time to relieve him. The Invisible Man showed no signs of being home, so Joe persuaded Maiko to go back to hall with him. He'd talked Maiko into joining him in a new game. Shell suspected that wasn't the only thing he had talked her into.

'You must have read about Water War,' Joe told Shell. 'Lots of people who were in the Spray game are playing. You have to join us.'

'I promised I'd help Mac out. So did you.'

'Not exactly,' Maiko pointed out. 'Helping him was your

idea.'

'If you say so,' Shell said. 'You and Joe will still help us trap The Invisible Man after the lecture tomorrow, won't you?'

'Of course.'

'Great. So why don't you tell me about this Water War game?'

'It's a mass battle. Two teams, in the park, a week on Saturday. People wear different-coloured wristbands, to show which side they're on. Do you want to join us?'

'I'll think about it,' Shell said. That weekend, Mac might be in the final of the Spray game. The Water War sounded like fun, but the Spray game was more important.

SECOND WEDNESDAY, MIDDAY – RIK

The Cartoonist's password turned out to be an unlucky number added to the name of a famous Austrian cartoonist, Brick13. Once Rik worked it out, his new friend said he knew how to get them both into the building.

'It's all a matter of charm,' Lol told Rik.

Lol had a toolbox with him. Standing by the entrance, he waved it at a woman who was leaving with a baby. She seemed distracted, but not so distracted that she didn't get a good eyeful of Lol on her way out. What they said about the good-looking was true, Rik realized. They had special privileges.

'I don't suppose you're plumbers,' the woman with the baby said, as Rik held the door open for her. 'The water pressure in the building is very low. I couldn't take a proper shower this morning.'

'Same all over the city,' Rik assured her. 'Nothing to do with the plumbing.'

Once they were in, he phoned Jen. 'I'm on my way up. Be ready to switch places with me in the alcove.'

'OK,' Jen said. 'I'm ready.'

'Sounds like you've got a plan worked out,' Lol told Rik.

'I'm still worried The Cartoonist will find Jen before I have time to get upstairs with my weapon,' Rik told him.

'What are you using, a destroyer?'

'Nah, I like those, but for an inside job like this, I really like the flash flood.'

'Good choice. Want any help up there?'

'Better not. I'm conspicuous enough at it is. And my uh . . . friend can distract the security cameras for me when she comes out of hiding.'

'OK. I'll wait outside so I don't raise any suspicions by hanging about here. But don't forget you promised to help me.'

'I never break a promise,' Rik said, as he got into the elevator. 'Whatever you need.'

On The Cartoonist's corridor, Rik found the alcove where Jen had set up. She was crouched by a tiny window. There was no room for Rik there as well, so they swapped places and laptops.

'He's definitely in?'

'Oh yes,' Jen said. 'Look at the screen. He's accessing his email at the moment.'

'OK,' Rik said. 'Time for him to notice us.'

As Jen took off her overall, Rik accessed The Cartoonist's bank account. Pity he couldn't access The Cartoonist's computer keychain for the password. The bank's security system wouldn't let the computer save it. Rik turned this to his advantage. He had several attempts at the password, which was bound to set off an alarm of some kind.

'OK,' he told Jen. 'Off you go.'

Jen took the back-up laptop and crouched in the corridor,

directly outside The Cartoonist's apartment. There was a security camera at the end of the corridor. The sight of a girl in an orange bikini, pretending to type, was bound to rouse even the sleepiest security camera operative. Rik hoped The Cartoonist would be alerted first. On the screen, a message came up from the guy's bank.

```
Your security is important to us. If
your next attempt to access your account
uses an incorrect password, your account
will be frozen. You will not be able to
access your account until you have reset
your password by telephone. Do you want
to continue?
```

Rik paused. An email would have been sent to The Cartoonist by now, asking him to confirm that he was trying to access his own account. All Rik needed was for The Cartoonist to realize that his wi-fi was being leeched from close by. So he needed to create a connection problem. Rik loaded an illegal bittorrent site. He typed in the name of the most popular new-release movies and selected the version with the largest file size. It had hundreds of seeders, which would make the download quick, as fast as The Cartoonist's bandwidth would allow. Rik clicked on *download*.

Megabytes poured into and out of his computer. If The Cartoonist was online, he would notice his connection speed slowing down to a trickle, like the water in Rik's tap that morning. Come on! This was meant to be a smart guy.

'Hey!'

Jen gave a little screech. It was happening. Rik pulled out his flash flood gun, which was primed and fully loaded. He heard The Cartoonist's voice, which he knew well. This guy was a famous TV personality, a game show host. And he wasn't alone.

'Move away from that laptop,' The Cartoonist said. 'For all I know, you might have a water balloon concealed in it.'

'Whatever you say,' Jen said.

'Are you my assassin?' the TV personality asked. 'Or a thief?'

'Neither,' Jen said. She took another step back. The Cartoonist picked up her laptop, examined it, then closed the lid. He put it down to one side. That was good. It belonged to the university and Rik would rather not get it wet. Rik poked his head out of the alcove into the corridor. The target had his back to him. Rik pointed the custom water pistol that Deniro had given him, the one with the long, narrow shaft and fat, stubby handpiece. Time to test its range.

'Why are you dressed like that?' The Cartoonist asked Jen.

'Because I wanted you to know that I wasn't carrying,' Jen said, as something poked out from The Cartoonist's door. 'And because I knew that I was going to get wet,' she added.

Jen hadn't noticed the mike yet, but Rik could guess what was going on. TV personalities didn't play street games unless there was something in it for them. And they didn't have TV cameras in their homes unless they were participating in a reality TV show. Rik nodded at his partner. Jen glanced at Rik for half a moment: just enough for The Cartoonist to sense that something was wrong. He looked back over his shoulder. Too late. Rik pressed the trigger. Water bounced off the bloke's expensive hair-piece, covering his glasses, soaking his T-shirt.

'Come on!' Rik called to Jen. 'He's making a TV show. Let's get out of here before they show the whole world what we look like!'

Jen picked up the laptop. Rik kicked The Cartoonist's door back so that the cameras wouldn't get a good look at him.

'Your laminate,' he said in a stern voice.

'Oh, you're good,' the TV star said. 'A glamorous girl in a bikini to distract me. That's very smart.'

'It was her idea,' Rik said, taking the target laminate.

'How about an interview?' called a voice from behind the door.

'Not until this is over,' Rik said. 'And don't follow me, or I'll soak all of your equipment, I swear!'

SECOND WEDNESDAY 12.11 P.M.
– HAN

Han waited at DC's block of flats. There was only a slim chance the cycle courier would return here, but she had to take it. Han wished she were old enough to drive, that she could wait in a car, maybe pull up alongside DC at some traffic lights, spray her on the road. Taxis were expensive, and buses gave you no flexibility. Nor did trams.

DC didn't return. Han observed a couple of people using bike lockers. These were over on the side of the building that was furthest from the river. Now Han knew where DC was likely to keep her bike. It should only be a matter of waiting. Sooner or later, she would be in a position to spray her. If DC ever came home.

The simplest way to stay safe in this game was to visit your home as little as possible. Han hadn't been back to her squat since Monday. Instead, she'd gone back to her real home. Mum thought that camp was over. Tonight Han was meant to be on a revision sleepover with a friend who would cover for her.

The idea came to Han out of the blue, the way the best ideas often do. DC was hard to track down because she had a vehicle that could go anywhere, that was flexible and not confined to any traffic system. Last night, Han had nicked Mum's back-up credit card, to use in an emergency. Now was the time to use it.

SECOND WEDNESDAY 12.13 P.M.
– RIK

'Did you recognize him?' Rik asked Jen on the elevator down. Rik was so excited, he wanted to hug Jen but didn't have the nerve. 'That isn't his real name on the laminate.'

'Maybe it is,' Jen said. 'TV people have made-up names, stage names.'

'True,' Rik said. 'Oh, I forgot, there's this guy downstairs. He helped me to get in. So I said we'd help him with his next kill.'

'I'll bet you did,' Jen muttered. 'Did you let him in?'

Rik could see that something was wrong. 'No. he's outside. What's going on, Jen? We just pulled off a superb hit. It'll be on TV. Even if I don't win, we'll be stars.'

'Being a star wasn't part of my plan,' Jen said. 'And I like you, Rik. That wasn't part of my plan either.'

They stepped out of the elevator.

'There he is,' Rik said. Lol was standing on the other side of the glass doors. Rik worried. How could he hope to win a girl like Jen when there was a guy as handsome as Lol around? He glanced at Jen to see how she reacted to Lol, but she was looking at the elevator display. Another lift was on its way down.

'That'll be the TV crew,' Rik said. 'Let's get out of here!'

'Don't you want to be famous?' Jen asked, even though she knew he didn't. 'You stay here. This one time, trust me.'

'What's going on?' Rik asked again. 'You know I don't want to be interviewed.' Full of adrenalin, he plucked up the courage to ask her what was on his mind. 'Am I missing something here? Don't you want to be seen with me?'

'It's not that. It's just . . .' Lol rapped on the glass door, indicating that they should come out. There was a bulge in the side of his overalls. Of course, he was kitted up.

Jen spoke in a rush. 'Listen, Rik. I already have a boyfriend. Him, out there. Lol's your assassin, not Drizzabone. When Lol was given you as a target, he got me to pretend I was a player, that you were my target. He even made up Drizzabone, put stuff about him on the game website. The idea was that I would find out if you had a difficult target, then lead Lol to you when you got an easy one.'

'I see,' Rik said. He ought to feel disgusted with himself, for trusting her. But he had suspected her motives from the start. Now, at least, her behaviour made sense. He had never had a chance with her. 'So it's all been an act, to help that guy out there win the game.'

'Lol's very persuasive. I thought it was just a game. Now I see how seriously you take it. I like you, Rik, I don't want to hurt you. So stay, be interviewed. I'll try and get rid of Lol, for now at least . . .'

The elevator door rang. The TV crew stepped out.

'Stay with me,' Rik asked Jen. 'Help me win.'

'How?' Jen asked, her voice plaintive, pained.

Rik shouted to the crew. 'OK, I'll do your interview. But before you do me, you really have to talk to that guy outside. He's the legendary Zorro. I was with him on his very first hit, when he took out a student called Maiko in the first minute of the game. You'd be mad not to interview him first!'

The crew, all six of them, charged out of the building, surrounding Lol.

'What's it going to be?' Rik asked Jen. 'Are you staying with him, or coming with me?'

SECOND THURSDAY 1.28 P.M. – MAC

Mac and Shell hung around the corridor outside the lecture theatre watching as students and lecturers straggled inside.

'This is so dangerous,' Shell told Mac. 'Suppose your assassin's in there? You've no idea what she looks like.'

'I suppose DC could be a student, but the chances of her knowing about this seminar are fairly low.'

'You say that, but a lot of people have gone in already.'

'Not our Invisible Man though.'

Mac's target hadn't stayed at his own house the night before. He and Shell had borrowed Joe's car and watched until two. Today, if The Invisible Man was in the university, he hadn't approached his office from the most obvious entrance. But the campus was a maze of buildings. This was going to be even more difficult than he'd feared.

A guy walked past, in typical student garb: jeans, sneakers, plain T-shirt. There was something familiar about him. Probably a customer from the burger bar. The guy went into the lecture theatre.

'We might as well go in now,' Shell said.

'You're sure nobody will know I'm not a student?'

'Believe me, you look the part.'

The lecture theatre was nearly full. The Invisible Man strode to the podium at exactly one-thirty, the lecture's start time. The Invisible Man's hair was cropped so close, it was hard to tell where his bald patch started and his real hair ended. He had a jutting jaw and wide, lively eyes. Beneath his sports jacket, he wore a pink, collarless shirt.

'*Whisky is for drinking, water is for fighting over*. Mark Twain said that in 1881, but it's never been more true than it is today. Clean water is at a premium. Water shortages bring disease, poverty, and untold damage. Rivers run through more than one country and when one country tries to divert a river, or build a dam that stops the water reaching another country, wars break out. In the last fifty years, there have been over five hundred conflicts between countries as a result of disagreements over water. All of which puts in perspective the hosepipe bans and four-minute showers the government is telling us to take. And it trivializes what I'm here to talk to you about today . . .'

Suddenly, The Invisible Man opened his jacket, to reveal a leather holster beneath his left shoulder. He brandished a slender black revolver. The audience gasped. They weren't used to seeing guns on campus. But Mac recognized the model at once. It was an old-school water pistol with a reloadable water magazine. The Invisible Man pressed the trigger and a jet of water crossed the room. The Invisible Man sprayed a 'no mobiles' notice on the far wall. It was a flashy, empty gesture. You weren't meant to use realistic guns in the spray game, for fear of panic on the streets. But The Invisible Man had his audience's attention. As the water dripped on to the lecture hall's tiled floor, there was some laughter and scattered applause. The Invisible Man warmed to his theme.

'Water is at the heart of our existence. We can't live without it. It covers four-fifths of our planet, yet we are always running short of it. And today, I want to talk to you about two games that provide a choice of metaphors for the place of water in the world today. One is an assassination game. The other is all-out warfare . . .'

SECOND THURSDAY 1.34 P.M.
– JEN

'I don't know what I'm doing here,' Jen told Rik as they jumped on to the bus. 'Lol's my boyfriend. We've been going out for two months.'

'Get off and go back to him if you want,' Rik said, but it was already too late. The bus was moving.

Jen didn't really want to get off. If she was honest with herself, looks aside, she liked Rik much more than she liked Lol. Half the girls in her school year thought Lol was God's gift. Of course, when he asked her out, she said yes. When he asked for her help in the Spray game, she did what he asked. Jen was lucky to be with him, everyone said that. In the league of good looks, she was an eight out of ten. If she made an effort, a nine. Lol was a ten verging on eleven.

'You saved me,' Rik said. 'I appreciate it, no matter what you did before. I never really bought it when you said you fancied me.'

'Lol could have sprayed you two days ago,' Jen told him. 'But then I told him your new target was The Cartoonist and you had a better chance of spraying him than he did. Lol could never have pulled off a stunt like the one we just did.

But he'd have done the assassination himself if he'd known the target was a celebrity. Lol really wants to be famous. He figures, with his looks, it's only a matter of time before some big TV deal comes knocking at his door. Winning the game would speed that up.'

'He's just had his TV interview,' Rik pointed out.

'I wouldn't put it past Lol to pretend he is Zorro,' Jen said with a smirk. 'Except, doesn't Zorro have a moustache?'

'A minor inconvenience,' Rik said. 'But I've met Zorro. He seemed like a nice guy to me. This Lol guy sounds like a user. So how come you're still going out with him?'

Jen didn't know how to answer this. 'Seems I'm not, any more. He's bound to dump me when he realizes I told you who he was.'

'Not if you dump him first.'

'You've got a point.' Jen got out her phone and texted Lol. CONSIDER YOURSELF DUMPED, LOSER! It felt good. She wouldn't miss him. But she'd miss the envious looks of other girls when she was out with him. What would those girls say if they saw her out with Rik? He was clever, and considerate, and funny, and cuddly. It would be a stretch to call him handsome, but his face had character.

'Who's on The Cartoonist's target laminate?' she asked Rik.

'I haven't had a chance to look yet.' He got it out. 'Uh-oh.'

'What is it?' Jen asked, with a sinking feeling. 'Someone you've heard of?'

'I knew I shouldn't have invoked his name earlier,' Rik

said, handing her the card. It showed a long-haired man with a pencil moustache. Zorro.

SECOND THURSDAY 2.13 P.M.
– MAC

'The basic aim of a Water War is to get your opponents as wet as possible. The game can be played by a huge number of people in a variety of ways – one hit kills, free for all, as a kind of tag. But a general principle holds: the side with the most dry members at the end is the one that wins. Water Wars resembles real warfare, with water substituting for blood.

'The world is short of water, but we would rather waste a small amount of water than spill a lot of blood. If only governments could agree to settle real wars with water pistols, think how many lives could be saved! Unfortunately, as we have already discussed, water is more likely to be the cause of wars than it is to be the solution.

'The other game, the one that I'm involved in at the moment, is known as Street Wars. Or, more poetically, Spray. Historically, it derives from a game called Assassins. This game is all about the individual. It's thought that Assassins was first played in universities, although the variant involving water weapons is more recent.

'Spray is a game designed by and for individuals. Some versions allow teamwork but the rules always specify that the team has to have a leader and if that leader is assassinated, the whole team is out. So it's really about individuals with a support network rather than a team. It's a very pure game, a competition that can only have one winner. It's a game that encourages deviousness, selfishness and, most of all, ingenuity. I'm writing a book about its history. But that's not my main motive for joining the game this year. My main motive, and that of the other players, is not to win. It's to have fun.'

There was mild applause, which the lecturer waved aside. 'We have time for a few questions.'

'How many people have you killed?' A girl at the front wanted to know.

'Four. That's one more than the average for people who've got this far in the game. Experience shows that anybody who doesn't have three hits by tomorrow will be eliminated from the game.'

'Who runs the game?'

'Somebody who calls himself the gamekeeper. At least, the person I met looked like a he. And the gamekeeper has assistants. There's some debate about whether it's always the same person throughout the game or whether the mantle of gamekeeper is passed on. I don't think this matters too much. The only thing is that, whoever does the role has to have independent means. The game's entry fees are low. The prize isn't very high either, but there must be a lot of expenses.'

'What's your name in this game?'

'I call myself "The Invisible Man" after the book by H.G. Wells, meaning that I hope not to be spotted. Although, giving a talk like this hardly helps my invisibility.'

There were polite chuckles. Can't be many jokes in university lectures, Mac figured, if they think that's funny. Shell waved her arm in the air and was called.

'Do you think your assassin is in the audience?' she asked.

'More than likely, but I've no way of knowing who my assassin is, until they spray me with a water pistol or soak me with a water balloon. At least I know that they can't get me in here. The rules are very clear. You can't soak person in their workplace – or their home, unless the target is foolish enough to invite the assassin inside.'

'Are you in this game to win?' Mac asked.

'There's no point in playing a game you don't intend to win,' The Invisible Man said. 'But the favourite has to be a player who calls himself "Zorro". He's won twice before. What he does is he moves to the game cities in order to qualify for the competition. He's very devious. He took out a student on this very campus in the first minute of the game.'

The Invisible Man described the double bluff that Zorro had used to take out Joe and Maiko. There was more laughter, then The Invisible Man looked at his watch. He pointed at a display on the digital whiteboard.

'Follow the game on the websites shown here if you're interested. And you can observe or even participate in the Water War game at the city park a week on Saturday. It's rare that you get two games going on at the same time, so make the most of it. Presuming, that is, you can get hold of enough water to fill your pistols.'

He grinned, then slammed a new magazine into his water pistol and took aim at the rear door.

'Remember, don't use realistic pistols like this on the street. They could easily raise a panic. Now, who dares leave first?'

SECOND FRIDAY 2.37 P.M. – RIK

Jen and Rik went for a swim at the crowded public pool, then returned to Rik's one-bedroom flat. He lived on a narrow street not far from campus. Luckily, the place wasn't too big a mess.

'I can't take out Zorro!' Rik moaned. He put on a German accent. 'For me, ze var is ofer.'

'Have more faith in yourself,' Jen said. 'It's better to have Zorro as your target than to have him as your assassin. You know who your assassin is, and he's no great shakes. I can help protect you from him.'

Rik looked at the laminate again. It told him Zorro's real name and address. His target even had a job, though Rik doubted he'd be there much. According to the laminate, Zorro was a systems analyst. His address was in one of the cheapest parts of the city – an area full of squats and derelict housing. It made for a good fake address. And a dangerous hunting ground.

'Didn't you meet him on day one?' Jen asked. 'At least you know what he looks like.'

She looked distracted. It was probably sinking in that she'd just dumped her handsome bastard of a boyfriend to hook up with a bloated porpoise. Rik mustn't let himself get too taken with Jen. He'd had crushes on girls before. Friendship soon turned to pity if he showed an unexpected romantic side. Embarrassment all round.

'According to the laminate, Zorro lives over on the west side,' he said. 'Public transport's terrible in that part of the city. Even with a taxi, we'll be vulnerable to Lol as soon as we get out into the street.'

'One thing about Lol,' Jen said. 'He's too lazy to learn to drive.'

'Unfortunately,' Rik said. 'The same thing goes for me.'

'But not me,' Jen said. 'I started lessons on my seventeenth birthday. Passed my test last week. Want to see if I can borrow my mum's car?'

SECOND FRIDAY 2.42 P.M. – MAC

Mac and Shell lingered in the grey corridor outside the lecture theatre, waiting for The Invisible Man to leave. Shell pretended to read a noticeboard. The guy who Mac had half recognized on the way in brushed past them on his way out. Something made Mac say hello.

'How're you doing?' The guy responded, as though he knew who Mac was.

'OK. What did you think of the lecture?'

'Pretty basic stuff. But that's universities for you. They're always years behind the time but like to think they're cutting edge.' He lowered his voice. 'Is he your target?'

Mac nodded.

'Have you got a plan to get him?'

'Not really,' Mac said. 'He's pretty secure here.'

'Only while he's inside,' the guy pointed out. 'You never know, he might fall for the old fire alarm trick. If you were a student here, that would get you into trouble, but . . . here he comes.'

Mac saw his chance.

'Who was that guy you were talking to?' Shell asked.

'I think he's another player,' Mac told her. 'He gave me an idea. See that cluster of people around The Invisible

154

Man? I want you to join them and . . .'

He lowered his voice. Shell listened, then hurried off to join the lecturer. The guy who had offered Mac the advice was already at the stairs. How did he know that Mac wasn't a student? The guy needed a haircut. His heavy black-rimmed glasses made it hard to get a good look at his face. Even so, Mac recognized him. He knew that voice. Of course. That was who he was! No wonder he was here.

The gamekeeper nodded to Mac before turning away. Mac gave him a half-smile in return. Then he broke the glass on the fire alarm.

SECOND FRIDAY 2.46 P.M. – HAN

Han's bike was highly weaponized. She had a water mortar on the back panier. It held half a dozen water balloons, any one of which could soak a target. She had a super-soaker clipped to the crossbar, where she could grab it and aim at a moment's notice. And she had a purple double-helix blaster strapped to her back, resting against her right shoulder. This was a big gun that didn't need pressurizing and had a decent range. Finally, for later use, in a holster beneath her left shoulder was what looked like a slim revolver, classically shaped. Oh yes, Han was well prepared. All she had to do was locate her target.

Han wanted to eliminate DC before the weekend was over, otherwise, she knew, the target might change. DC had made only one kill, on the first day. If she was going to get another by tomorrow night, she would have to move sharpish. The way Han saw it, DC must have been given a very difficult target. This close to the wire, she was bound to take risks to get her or him. Risks that exposed her.

Han had another target, too. She must have shown Chris's photo to a thousand people. One or two recognized him. A couple said he had served them in a bar. One claimed he worked in a restaurant. No solid details.

Three people – each a student – reckoned he'd served them a burger, though none was certain where. Han had twice toured the fast food places around the university campus, with no sign of Chris. This afternoon, short of other ideas, she decided to go into them one more time.

On her third stop, she got lucky. A guy who called himself Ben.

'Is this an old photo of my mate, Mac? He worked here until a few days ago.'

'He did? Why did he leave?'

'You're in the game, right?'

'Uh, yeah.'

'And that's your bike outside?'

'Yes.'

'You look smaller than you do on the bike, but it's you? DC?'

'Oh. No.' Han didn't know what to say. She'd struck lucky. DC was her target. This 'Mac' was DC's target. She was only one kill away from him. 'I'm not her.'

'Then how do you know it's a her, huh? Mac wasn't sure.'

'Because . . . look, I'm an old friend of his. Do you have an address, or a mobile number?'

'Don't they give you that info on the target laminate?'

'They do. But he's not my target, honest. He's . . .'

Her voice dribbled off and Ben interrupted.

'Thing is, I promised Mac I wouldn't give anyone any info about him. He's got this grungy little flat but it wouldn't help you to know where it is, because he's never there.'

'Never?'

'Are you sure you're not his assassin?'

'No. Of course not.' Han got out her target laminate and showed it to Ben. 'See? I'm after the person who's after him.'

Ben still didn't look convinced. 'You look a little young to be playing the game. Isn't it for sixteen and overs?'

'I am sixteen,' Han insisted. 'And a half,' she added, feeling foolish as the words came out. Ben didn't look convinced. In daylight, without make-up, Han barely looked her real age, which was fifteen.

'And you say you're an old friend of Mac's?'

'That's right,' Han said.

'Tell you what. I get off at eight tonight. Meet me for a drink and I'll give Mac a ring, see if he's willing to meet you.'

'Great. Where?'

They agreed a café to meet in. Han wasn't sure she'd make it. She'd found out three things: 1. Chris was calling himself Mac. 2. He was still in the game, and: 3. His assassin was DC. If Han got to DC, she would get to Chris. She had to find her this afternoon. She had to.

SECOND FRIDAY 2.51 P.M.
– SHELL

Shell knew two things about fire alarms. The first was that, when a fire alarm sounded, everybody was supposed to go to a specific place. The second was that nobody ever knew where that specific place was. As the alarm screeched, deafeningly, through the university's echoey corridors, people scattered in different directions. The Invisible Man still had a crowd of students around him, including Shell. She glanced in the direction that she had last seen Mac in, but he wasn't there. Which was good. Mac had to follow The Invisible Man outside, but not too obviously. The Invisible Man mustn't spot him. If necessary, Shell could always ring Mac to let him know where his target was standing.

'Which way?' she asked The Invisible Man, who was grinning as though he had set off the fire alarm himself. He consulted a sign.

'Follow me!' he called. The Invisible Man guided Shell and a group of students down a stairwell. At the bottom was an exit that opened into a loading area. The Invisible Man held the door open for his fan club.

Shell contrived to be the last one out. As she went through the door, she turned to thank the lecturer. But he was already slipping away, heading back towards where he'd come from.

'Hey!' she said. 'You can't go back in there.'

He gave her a sly grin. 'I'm invisible. I have to disappear.'

Shell tried to stall him. 'Doesn't it show more skill to disappear outside than it does in here, where nobody's allowed to spray you?'

'Good point, but—' The lecturer was interrupted by what appeared to be a uni security officer, in his distinctive green, short-sleeved shirt.

'Everyone outside, please. No exceptions. Outside. Now!'

'Show me your bag, would you?' The Invisible Man asked Shell. 'I just want to be sure you're not my assassin.'

'If you don't mind, sir, I need you outside now!' The security officer was younger than the retired police officers who usually did the job, but he had the polite yet firm manner off pat. The Invisible Man didn't challenge him. Having seen that Shell wasn't carrying, the lecturer allowed the security officer to herd him outside. In the hot air, he nervously scanned their surroundings, looking for any sign of his assassin.

'Would you like me to escort you to your car, sir?' the security officer asked.

'That won't be necessary,' The Invisible Man said. 'If you could just tell me how far I am from the main entrance car park.'

'Certainly, sir. Let me show you on this map.' As Mac reached into his capacious pockets, The Invisible Man appeared to notice that the officer's loose, grey trousers didn't match his shirt. Shell had been wondering how long it would take him to catch on. Too long. There was no time for him to run. Mac already had the water pistol in his hand.

'You devious . . .'

Mac sprayed the guy's pink, collarless shirt, the water hitting so hard that the hairs in the lecturer's chest showed through the thin fabric.

'Enough, enough!' A few of the students from the lecture were still around. A moment ago, they had been hanging on the lecturer's every word. Now they looked back and giggled.

'Your laminate, please,' Mac said.

'That was so cool,' Shell told him. 'Where did you get that shirt and clipboard?'

'The storage cupboard I ducked into after sounding the alarm.'

'The university will not look kindly on your behaviour this afternoon,' the lecturer told Mac, handing him his card.

'What makes you think I'm a student?' Mac said, taking off his security officer shirt and throwing it to the ground.

SECOND SATURDAY 9.02 A.M. – HAN

GAMEKEEPER COMMUNIQUE NUMBER 2

Return-Path: <gamekeeper@assassins.org.uk>
Received: from aamtain07-winn.ispmail.nobody
.com ([81.103.221.35]) for <addresslist
concealed>; 76.00.36 +0800

Eleven days gone and the final week is
almost upon us. Most of you receiving
this are serious players with three or
four kills under your belt. Some have
significantly more. Time to get down to
the nitty gritty. If you don't have
three kills by midnight tonight, I don't
care how tough your target is, you're
out. Keep your laminate as a souvenir –
there'll be new ones for the players who
make it through to the final week. They
can expect an email tomorrow.

Han closed her email and looked out of the train window.

She had no idea who her new assassin was. That student had come close, but not close enough, and she had avoided the squat since then. Last night, Han had gone home, and now she was about to take the train back into the city. Mum thought she was having a shopping day. Mum was easy to fool, mainly because she was home so little herself.

Yesterday, Han had wasted the whole day searching for her target. Last night, she'd stood up Ben. She'd thought the scenario through and meeting him wouldn't work. Before he gave out the address, Ben was bound to call Chris on his mobile. He'd put Han on the line. That wasn't how she wanted to encounter him, not after all this time. Suppose he rejected her, refused to meet? No. Han wanted to meet Chris face to face, without warning.

DC would have received the same email from the gamekeeper. She would be after Mac, as Chris called himself. Han hoped to get to her before she left her flat. But if she couldn't, it didn't matter much. For yesterday, before she went home, Han had broken into DC's bike locker. She didn't take anything. But she did leave something behind.

SECOND SATURDAY 10.08 A.M. – SHELL

Shell and Mac ate a late breakfast in the corridor's small kitchen. Outside, the sky was a steely blue. It was going to be another really hot one.

'Why do you keep looking at the road?' Shell asked.

'I keep expecting to see a cyclist coming for me. DC has to get me today, or be eliminated.'

'Maybe you're being paranoid,' Shell said. 'Could be DC's given up. She or he's waiting to be eliminated from the game. So it's tomorrow you need to worry. When you get a new assassin.'

'There can't be that many players left,' Mac said. 'With my luck, I'll get Zorro.'

Shell examined Mac's new target laminate.

'This one doesn't sound too difficult.'

'Everybody's difficult at this stage. If a player's lasted this long, they have to be good.'

'Yes,' Shell said. 'But you're better.'

'No, I'm just lucky. If I hadn't met you . . .'

He looked at her and Shell beamed at him. Maybe this was the moment when he'd say something romantic. She'd spent ages doing her hair this morning, then chosen her most flattering clothes, even though she was liable to get soaked. But Mac seemed not to notice. There had been no follow up to their kiss, which was days ago. He seemed immune to physical attraction. She didn't think he was gay. She'd never seen him glance at a guy with a flicker of interest. Maybe he was a late developer. Or it could be he already had a girlfriend, hiding in his mysterious past.

A week ago, Shell could have got off with Joe, but he was with Maiko now. And who could blame him for picking her? Shell had made her interest in Mac clear. Maybe she'd made the wrong choice.

'Have you got your super-soaker ready?' she asked Mac.

'Primed for action,' he said, glancing once more at the laminate before putting it in his wallet. 'Let's go.'

SECOND SATURDAY 11.21 A.M.
– HAN

DC was on the move again. Han watched her navigate her way across the city on her laptop. Han had chosen the cafe' she was sitting in because it was central. If DC took an obvious route, Han might be able to intercept her. You could really nip around on a bicycle.

The GPS device Han had hidden under DC's rear mudguard was the one Mum planted on the car of her second husband when he was playing around. The day he left home, there was no note, only the round metal tracker on the table in the hall. He knew. Han took it. Partly to save Mum an extra humiliation. And partly because she thought the transponder might come in useful one day.

Han was all Mum had left. Mum was terrified of driving her away. She'd been given all kinds of freedom. No checking up on her when she pretended to be staying with friends, or off on spurious trips. This evening, if Han hadn't sprayed DC by then, she'd be out with a fictitious friend, whose home she'd stay in overnight.

Was DC stalking Chris, or making bike deliveries? She went past the same place twice, stopping for five minutes each time. Han took a note of the approximate address. It could be where Chris lived.

Han was paranoid that her own assassin would be getting as busy as she was. He or she had been on the job for six days. Han had only been back to the flat once in that time. She could be reported for breaking the rules. But she had read through the archived messages of previous tournaments. Players didn't tend to be thrown out for breaking residency rules. Other rules, yes, including the one about age. That could disqualify her at any time.

DC had been stopped in the university for more than five minutes. Not too far to ride. Han paid for her coffee and slid her laptop into her backpack, where it nestled next to her reserve super-soaker. She put on her white face mask. More and more people were wearing these because of pollution and super bugs. Together with the cycle helmet, it did a really good job of disguising her.

SECOND SATURDAY 11.25 A.M.
– MAC

Mac felt conspicuous, walking around with a super-soaker in his hand. Shell, similarly armed, was to his left, Maiko to his right. Most guys would pay a small fortune to have two such attractive girls as their entourage. But Mac wasn't most guys. He was in this city to win, not to get a girlfriend.

'Look out!' Shell said. 'Behind!'

Maiko was meant to be watching the rear. Mac swivelled round, but it was too late. A torrent of brackish water sprayed him, soaking his T-shirt, trickling down into his jeans. He swore.

'This water's filthy! You're meant to use clean!'

'It's recycled shower water from the water butts,' Joe explained. 'If we'd tried to fill the super-soakers from taps, we'd have been there all day. The pressure's way down again.'

'We managed to fill ours!' Maiko said, pushing the shaft of her double-helix gun so that it pummelled a picturesque spray at Joe.

'I'll get you back!' Joe insisted, pointing his super-soaker at her. But he had used most of his water already and had forgotten to pump the pressure back up. All that came out was a pitiful stream. The spray dribbled to the dry ground before it could reach Maiko.

Joe and Maiko were practising for the Water War. It gave them an excuse to use the super-soakers they'd bought a fortnight before. Was it less than a fortnight since the game began? It felt longer to Shell. A fortnight ago, she didn't know that Mac existed. Now she was, at most, a week away from losing him.

'Isn't this more fun than an assassination game? Joe asked Mac. Both of them were dripping wet, but looked happy.

'I prefer games that have winners and losers,' Mac said. 'In this game, everybody gets wet.'

As if to prove his point, a bunch of male students charged on to the lawn. They carried a variety of water weapons and were whooping like they were at a big gig or a cup final. One of them saw the two dry girls with the two wet boys. He aimed his CPS.

'Look out!' Shell called. She got behind the two boys, who took the brunt of the spray aimed at her. Maiko wasn't so lucky. She was soaked from head to toe. The group of guys ran off laughing. Shell aimed a torrent at the one who had shot at her and Maiko, but only caught him on the shoulder.

'We'll have you next Saturday!' Joe yelled at them, then turned to the others. 'I'm going to reload.'

'I'm going to get changed,' Maiko said. 'Back in five mins.'

Shell looked at Mac. He seemed distracted.

'What's wrong?' she asked him. 'Want to go in and put on some dry stuff? I expect Joe could lend you some clothes.'

'No thanks,' Mac said. 'I'll dry off soon enough in this

heat. I'm worried because there are too many cyclists on the path over there. It makes me nervous.'

'You're out of range, standing here. But maybe we should get after your target,' Shell suggested.

'I told Joe we'd hang with him and Maiko for an hour, then he's going to give us a lift.'

'We could always catch a bus,' Shell said.

'I'd feel more comfortable in a car. You're more in control.'

'How did you plan to play this game before you met us?' Shell asked.

'On foot, if necessary. But this is more fun.' He gave her a wry smile. 'You ought to refill your super-soaker.'

'I don't think so,' Shell said. 'We're wasting time.'

'It's only a game,' Mac reminded her. 'We're just passing the time. One game's as good as another for getting through the day.'

Maiko returned, wearing a dry T-shirt. She waved at Joe, who was trying to reload his weapon from the water fountain. The trickle of discoloured liquid coming from the fountain was pitifully thin.

'OK,' Shell said. 'Let's play.'

SECOND SATURDAY 11.38 A.M.
– HAN

Han made good time across the city, but not good enough. While cycling, she wasn't connected. She didn't know where DC was. Han would have to find a wi-fi hot spot before she could check the transponder she'd planted on DC's bike. The weapon under Han's arm used to belong to her stepdad. Han had hidden the revolver because she was worried about what he'd do with it. Now she had her own plans. Earlier, she'd observed DC going back and forth in the part of the city she was entering now. This area consisted entirely of university students' halls of residence. DC was unlikely to be on a delivery. She'd be stalking her target. If Han cycled around the same circuit, she might happen upon her.

There was a big water fight next week. Han had seen posters for it. There were people with water pistols everywhere, practising. Heatwave foolishness. You expected to see kids having water fights, but these were meant to be the country's brightest young adults. Shouldn't they be in an air-conditioned library somewhere? Still, their frantic activity provided Han with good cover.

Why was DC stalking Chris here? Surely he wasn't a student? That said, DC was clever enough to be in the right place. Han wouldn't put it past Chris to fake an ID. Maybe the real Mac was somebody whose identity Chris had stolen. That could be how he'd disappeared off the face of the earth so completely.

Han came to the end of the halls of residence. Next to them was a large car park. Amazing how, in a city with a great public transport network, so many of the students had cars. You got around quicker on a bike. Today proved that. And cycling was healthier than driving. Messier, though. Han had been cycling frantically and the sweat was pouring down her back. Time to take off her mask and wipe her face, which was sticky and dirty and felt gross.

There she was! Han's target was stationary, at the edge of the car park, hidden behind a purple car. What was DC watching?

Han had no time to waste. She remounted her bike and cycled down the next lane to the one where DC was waiting. Her super-soaker was in position, fully primed. Chances were, she could spray her now, no trouble. But Han wanted to see DC's target first. She wanted to see her brother.

SECOND SATURDAY 11.42 A.M.
– MAC

Maiko, Shell and Joe escorted Mac to the car in classic entourage style: Joe in front, with Shell and Maiko flanking Mac. Cars posed a special danger to Mac. An assassin could hide in one or behind one. Joe's car was at the near end of the car park.

'Looks clear,' Joe said, scanning the people within range.

'How can you be sure?' Shell asked. 'Mac's assassin might have changed twice since he was stalked by the cyclist. It could be that middle-aged guy over there, talking to a student. Or that girl behind the SUV, the one wearing a face mask.'

'What girl?' Maiko asked. 'I don't see her.'

They reached Joe's red Hyundai.

'Let's just get in the car,' Mac said.

Joe opened the driver's door and Shell opened the passenger door. She pushed the passenger seat down. This was the moment when Mac was most exposed. He had to clamber over the lowered seat to get in the back. Shell glanced at the girl in the face mask. For a moment, their eyes met. Then the girl looked away. Shell followed her gaze.

'Get down!' she told Mac, pushing him to the concrete

floor. There, only twenty metres away from them, stood DC. The cyclist, in grey jeans and T-shirt, was pointing a super-soaker in Mac's direction. She was in range, but did she have a clear shot? Not if Shell and Maiko blocked Mac. Shell grabbed her friend. Both of them stood over Mac. DC hesitated. Was he or she going to try and come closer? Then something else happened.

The spray of water was sudden, swift and definitive. One moment DC was pointing her super-soaker. The next she was drenched from head to toe, sparkling with water and shaking her head in order to see her assassin. That was when she took off her helmet. Now Shell could see that DC was a woman, mid-twenties maybe. And she had been taken out by a girl. The other cyclist, the one in the face mask, who was approaching her, barely looked old enough to be in the game. But she was.

Joe started the engine.

'You're safe,' Shell told Mac, who was in the back of the car.

'Until the new assassin gets the laminate,' Mac said. 'Quick, get in! I want a look at her.'

Shell joined Mac in the back. Maiko took the front passenger seat. Joe began to drive in the direction of the wet woman cyclist.

'You two had me covered,' Mac said. 'Thanks.'

They got close to where the girl was talking to the woman. Face Mask had her back to the car. She and DC were between two cars, so Shell couldn't see her properly. Joe sounded his horn, trying to get the new assassin to turn round. DC scowled at all three of them, then gave Joe's windscreen a blast with her super-soaker. Face Mask glanced over her shoulder to see what was happening, but with her mask and helmet, it was hard to tell how much hair she had, never mind what her face looked like.

'I've swapped one dangerous cyclist for another,' Mac said. 'Come on, let's get out of here.'

'She knows where I've been staying,' Mac said, once they were on the main road. 'I need a new bolt hole for the final week.'

Shell's heart sank. This could be their last afternoon together.

SECOND SATURDAY 11.45 A.M. – HAN

Han glanced back as the red car left the car park. She knew the car's number plates, and she had got a good look at Chris's friends, who appeared to be students. Her brother was her target now. She would track him down in good time, especially if she recovered the transponder. DC stood up.

'Do you know how long I've been tracking him?' she asked Han. 'Since the second day of the game. I nearly had him then. But he's really hard to catch.'

'You were pretty tricky too,' Han said.

'You're a fool. If you'd waited a minute, until I sprayed him, then you'd have been given a new target, probably an easier one. Whereas now, Mac's seen you. He'll be even harder to catch.'

'I'm no fool,' Han said, reaching under the panier of DC's bike and pulling out the little tracking device. 'See?'

'You're resourceful, but you'll have trouble pinning that to him. He doesn't have a bike, or a car. Don't bother going to his flat. He's never there. And he's packed in his job.'

'Then how did you find him?'

'He sprayed a university lecturer yesterday. There was loads of discussion about it on the game talkboards. It sounded like he had help, so I figured he was hanging out with students.' DC reached into her back pocket. 'Here.' She handed over the laminate.

'Thanks.'

'Aren't you a bit young to be playing this game?'

'Aren't you a bit old?'

Han glanced at the details on the laminate. Not a word on there was true. Chris was always sneaky when it came to playing games.

SECOND SUNDAY 8.56 A.M. – GAMEKEEPER

The gamekeeper finished checking his email. The midnight deadline meant there had been frantic activity yesterday. Players eliminated all over the place. This morning, he had only to send out three emails, removing players from the game. Then three more emails, assigning new targets. He would deliver the new target laminates shortly, for, at this stage of the game, every hour was crucial.

Less than two weeks in, there were just twelve players left: six per cent of the original entry. The game might not last a full third week. Hard to tell. Sometimes, this stage of the game lingered. The cagier players who remained took so many precautions that none of them were able to get near each other. Gridlock. If that happened, the gamekeeper had to engineer a final game shoot-out, sometimes with himself as the target. The gamekeeper tweaked the rules every time, improving the experience. This time, by eliminating players without multiple hits, he had made such a gridlocked ending less likely.

There were some very good players left. Zorro, as a past winner, had to be the favourite, but Rik was sharp, for a first timer, and the mysterious Mac intrigued him. Then there was Han. His assistant said she might be underage, with a faked ID. But if you were clever enough to fake your way in, you were clever enough to play the game. Senile was the game's oldest player, although he might not be in the game for long, being Zorro's next target. The full target and assassin list looked like this:

Han - Mac
Mac - Badmonkey
Rik - Zorro
Keno - Peg
Zorro - Senile
Senile - Han
Conifer - Psycho
Peg - Lol
Psycho - Conifer
Conifer - Ran
Lol - Rik
Badmonkey - Keno

Would these last players fall quickly? The contests he liked best were ones where there was a clear winner, without his intervention. Some juggling of targets was always required in the final week, to ensure that there was only one winner. But he had a hunch. The game could be over by tomorrow evening.

SECOND SUNDAY 1.06 P.M. – RIK

Rik and Jen sat in her car, watching the flat where Zorro was supposed to be staying. There had been no sign of him since they showed up, yesterday evening. Jen had twice tried the door, with a convincing story at the ready. No response.

Rik didn't mind. This was the first night he had spent alone with a girl. At ten, she'd phoned her parents, said she was staying at a mate's. Jen was such a good liar. They'd stayed up all night, talking, then agreed to take turns to nap. Jen dozed, her head resting on Rik's right shoulder. It felt intimate, comfortable. It felt right.

Someone turned on to the street and Rik slid down his seat, jerking Jen awake.

'Is it him?' she asked, as a thin man crossed the street.

'I don't think so.' Rik had seen Zorro up close. He'd had a good look at his long hair and moustache and didn't think that they were fake. But this guy was the right age and build. He could have had a haircut and a shave.

'It could be him,' Rik said.

'Then don't take chances. Spray him!'

She was right. If the thin man went to the right building, Rik would jump out of the car and . . . and . . .

Suppose it was a double bluff? Suppose Lol was watching

their car and had sent a decoy over to draw them out? Lol knew Jen's car. The thin man turned a corner, heading away from the flat. Not Zorro.

'I'm thirsty,' Jen said. 'The water bottle's empty.'

They had been stuffed in this car for seventeen hours solid. They probably reeked. But Rik felt great. He'd stay another seventeen hours, if that was what Jen wanted. But if she wanted a drink, fine. This was only a game. He'd made it to the last week. He'd met Jen, and that counted for more than winning.

'He's not coming back,' Rik said. 'That's presuming he lives here at all. Let's go back to mine for a shower and lunch.'

'What about Lol? Jen said. 'Won't he be waiting there?'

'With any luck, Lol is Zorro's target and he's taken him out.'

'How would that work?' Jen asked, starting the engine. 'Say Zorro sprayed Lol then got you as a target and sprayed you, too? Would he win, even though there are other players left in the game?'

'Doubt it,' Rik said.

'It's meant to be last person standing, so I suppose he'd be given a new target laminate. Hold on, I need to stop for petrol.'

They pulled up at the petrol station.

'Pick up a bottle of water, too,' Rik suggested.

When she got back into the car she handed him a can of cola.

'No water left.' She handed him a copy of the city newspaper. *Water supplies limited to four hours a day* the headline said.

181

When they got back to Rik's flat, the coast was clear. He tried to make coffee. No water came from the tap. The paper didn't lie.

'So much for our showers,' Rik said. 'Does the paper say when the water's coming on?'

'It varies from area to area,' Jen told him. 'According to this, we could be rationed to two hours a day by next weekend. That's if it doesn't rain this week.'

'Should make the end of the game interesting,' Rik told her, pouring the last of his bottled water into the electric kettle.

SECOND SUNDAY 1.06 P.M. – HAN

'Han! Lunch!' This was Mum's fourth exasperated yell. Han was having a long lie in. She needed to conserve her energy to catch Chris. Later, she would do some homework, to get back in her teachers' good books. Her plan this week was to show up for registration and skive off only when she had a lead on Chris. She had no idea who her own assassin was, but the likelihood was she'd just had a new one assigned. School was a good place to hide.

'You're late,' Mum said, when Han finally came down.

'At least I'm here,' Han pointed out, as her little brother began to throw his chopsticks from his highchair.

'I don't suppose there's any point in asking what you've been up to all week?'

'Not really.'

'These stories about school friends and camps and homework aren't very convincing, you know. I remember what it was like to be your age. I know you're seeing a boy.'

'If you already know, you don't need to ask me, do you?'

'You don't deny it, then?'

'Want to see the news,' Han said, turning on the TV. She wished she could change the conversation as easily as she could the TV channel.

'Not while we're eating,' Mum said, taking the remote from Han. A commercial break ended and the local news began.

Organizers may be forced to cancel what is billed as the world's biggest ever water fight, scheduled to take place in City Park this coming Saturday. The reason: a water shortage that has reduced most parts of the city to just four hours a day of water. Organizers admit that playing the game might be in 'bad taste' during the current drought but say that, currently, they plan to go ahead with all players using recycled water.

Meanwhile, the water gun assassination game that has seen high jinks all over the city for the last fortnight is due to end this week.

Mum glanced at the screen as she piled noodles on to Han's plate. She seemed to have forgotten about turning the TV off.

'Do you remember how you and your brother used to play with water pistols all the time?' she asked Han.

'Sure,' Han said awkwardly. She and Mum never discussed Chris, not since he left home.

The game has drawn players of all ages and backgrounds, from students to TV personalities.

The screen showed a game show host being sprayed by someone out of shot. The celebrity began to plug a TV documentary about his involvement in the game.

'Chris would have loved this game,' Mum said, as the screen showed players spraying and being sprayed. Their shots didn't look real. There was nothing at stake in them. The players – if they really were players – were hamming it up for the camera.

We tried to get an interview with the game's mysterious organizer, who calls himself The Gamekeeper but he insists that he will give no interviews until the contest is over, and won't reveal how many players remain to be eliminated. Who are the favourites? Two of the last three contests have been won by the same player, who calls himself Zorro.

The screen cut to images of a thin, long-haired guy at an end of game party. He had a pencil moustache and a sly smile. Then the picture cut to an Architecture student called Joe, who described how Zorro had taken him out in the first minute of the game. Han recognized Joe. He was the guy she'd seen driving Chris around.

'Zorro's a legend in the game, but there's a player called Mac who I think can beat him. He's got the kind of—'

'Eat your noodles!' Mum said. 'You're thin enough as it is.' She muted the TV, cutting off Joe in mid-flow. Mum had made no connection between Han's long, recent absences and the report they'd just been watching. Good. Han stuffed a prawn into her mouth.

'I'm staying over at Chi's tonight,' she said, looking at her food rather than her mother. 'I'll go to school from there tomorrow.'

'If you say so,' Mum said. 'But be warned, I'm seeing the

head teacher on Tuesday. She's asked me to come in. It better not be about your attendance. You've got important exams coming up.'

WEEK THREE

THIRD MONDAY, 10.03 A.M. – RIK

Rik was at work. He could have taken a day's holiday, but half term was over and Jen had to be at school. She'd already phoned him to say that Lol was at school, too. Rik was safe. For now.

Zorro could be anywhere in the city. Without Jen's car, there was no point in Rik hanging around near his target's flat. Even if Zorro went there, Rik was way too conspicuous. So he did what he did whenever he wasn't out on call. He surfed the net, reading up on Zorro's past exploits, looking for clues on how to catch him.

Zorro wasn't like some of the other players. He wasn't boastful about his kills. He let his legend be built up by the people he sprayed.

One moment the street was empty. I turned around and he was right behind me.

A high-security building, the highest. But he managed to get a job as a security guard.

The moustache should have been a giveaway, but it was a fancy dress party and he had the figure of a woman. No prizes for

Zorro's moustache was a constant. The long hair was sometimes tied back, or hidden under a shirt. He was good at getting people to invite him in to their homes, and it seemed he really did work in IT. He's like my mirror image, Rik thought, a thin, hairy version of me. Rik scanned the most recent postings on the game website. There was a blog where active players recounted their exploits. When he clicked on 'refresh' a new entry appeared. The author called himself 'Senile'.

Looks like my days are numbered Senile wrote. *I spotted Zorro in the complex today, dressed as an orderly. He's not allowed to spray me here, but can get me any time I leave. So I'm stuck inside, with no chance of spraying my target. He'll get me sooner or later, but I plan to make him wait. Anyone got any advice on how to escape this creep?*

Rik sent Senile a private message. It ended *We might be able to help each other, but once he knows that you know, we're in trouble. Delete your blog entry.* Then he waited. There was a call. He had to visit one of the university IT centres, replace a frozen monitor. When he got back, he pressed 'refresh'. Senile's entry about Zorro was gone. Rik checked his email. Senile had sent his phone, address and room number. Rik emailed the gamekeeper, asking for a rule clarification. Then he texted Jen. Lol was still in school. Rik was safe to leave. He called a taxi. Finally, he phoned his boss.

'Need to take some personal time. Got to visit this really old guy in a home on the other side of town. He's in trouble.'

'A relative?' the head of IT asked.

'Even closer than that,' Rik said, and hung up.

As he waited for the taxi, Rik checked his email and thought about texting Jen a third time, telling her where he was going. But suppose, now that they were back at school together, Lol had already persuaded Jen to go out with him again? He might get hold of her messages. Did Rik trust Jen to stay with him? Best, he decided, not to test that. He would call Jen again only when he needed her. Best of all, he would call her when he had eliminated Zorro.

THIRD MONDAY 1.13 P.M. – MAC

Mac stood on a busy corner in the business district, sweating heavily, watching the street. Last night he'd dreamt of a girl on a bicycle. He'd never dreamt about DC, but the girl who'd sprayed DC, she was different. She was something. She was going to spray him. He'd only seen her from behind, yet sensed at once that she would eliminate him from the game. Spooky. His new assassin knew where he lived. And she knew where he had been hiding. Mac had nowhere to go.

There he was, Mac's new target. Crossing the road in his lunch hour, not a care in the world. He wore a Beatles 'mop top' wig – that was, unless his hair had grown a great deal since the photo on the target laminate. It wasn't much of a disguise. In fact, it drew attention to him. The player's name, Badmonkey, suggested he didn't take the game too seriously. In which case, how come he had got this far?

Mac relaxed. All he had to do was cross the road, catch his target up, spray him from behind, take his laminate and get back in Joe's car, which was waiting down the road. It was really good of Joe, Maiko and Shell to keep helping him. Mac liked Shell. If things were different, he might get something going with her.

The light changed. Mac crossed the road, walked past the

busy shops along the dry street. In this part of the city, where serious money was made, everything looked clean, but the air still reeked of takeaways and drains. Rats scuttled along the gutters. Badmonkey turned a corner at the end of the block. His office was another two blocks away. Mac had time to catch him up and spray him before he reached the exclusion zone, which was anywhere within one block of his workplace.

'Hey! Let go!' Arms lifted Mac. They belonged to two guys in their twenties. Both looked like body-builders, bodyguards, or both.

'Turn around, pal. Make tracks.'

'You work for Badmonkey?'

The men turned Mac so that he was facing in the opposite direction. Then they put him back on the ground. A young woman stood in front of him. She was dressed in classic office garb, grey flannel skirt and jacket, despite the heat. And she was taking photos of him with a digital camera. One of the thugs spoke.

'None of your business who we work for, pal, but you're not wanted around here. Now get lost. Understood?'

'Understood.'

It was already too late for Mac to catch his target. He started walking away from the bodyguards and the photographer. This one was going to be harder than he'd thought.

THIRD MONDAY 1.15 P.M. – HAN

After afternoon registration, Han slipped out of school and caught the train into the city. She had handed in her homework earlier, and placated teachers whose lessons she'd missed the week before half term. There would still be trouble when Mum went to see the Head. Han couldn't decide how to play that one. She could be all sweetness and light and lie through her teeth. Or she could go AWOL.

Growing up, Han idolized her big brother. Dad was always working. Chris was always around, looking after her when Mum was busy, playing with her. Some days, he put her before school and his friends. Then Dad left. Chris became remote – more so when Mum met someone new, so quickly, and proceeded to marry him. (OK, Han wasn't stupid. She eventually worked out that Mum was already seeing husband number two and he was the reason why Dad left.)

Han was only a kid. She cleaved to her new stepdad. Chris, as soon as he turned sixteen, went to live with his father. There was nothing Mum could do. *Your brother will come back in time*, Mum had said. Han wasn't convinced, even then. Now, all this time later, he was still gone. So was her real dad. He'd been dead for two years. Han didn't find out until after the funeral.

The flat was as she'd left it. No sign that anyone was watching. Han checked the game's website. Reading between the lines, there weren't many players left. Nobody had written about DC being sprayed yet. A couple of people were talking about Mac as a potential winner, after he got The Invisible Man, but he only had three kills, compared to Han's five. Zorro remained the favourite, with six kills. Badmonkey, who seemed to have come from nowhere, had the same number.

There were no new emails from the gamekeeper. No mail of any kind waiting for Han. Good. She hadn't been sussed.

Who was Mac's target? If Han knew that, she would know where to look for him, but the website offered no clue. This was an impossible game, Han decided. How could you win it without a team, or at least a bunch of helpers, as Chris had? Funny. Her brother had never been terribly good at making friends. He was a loner, like her. He used to say she was his only friend. And then she wasn't.

Time to get out. Han's assassin would be watching this place. She phoned for a taxi, requesting the woman driver who had picked her up before. The driver would know to park directly outside the door, keeping Han covered. Han would go to the station, where, earlier, she had left her bike in a lock up. Then she would comb the city, paying particular attention to the university, looking for Chris.

THIRD MONDAY 1.25 P.M. – RIK

Rik stayed outside the complex, watching through an open door. The second lunch sitting was winding down. No sign of Zorro. Rik didn't want to alert the target to his presence. Zorro was bound to recognize him from their encounter on day one. He would know why Rik was there. If Rik didn't take him by surprise, he'd be gone before Rik got close enough to spray him.

The name Senile worried Rik a little. Was it a joke, or a confession? Rik's grandparents were in their mid-sixties. He was used to being around old people. But most of the people in the dining area looked considerably older than his grandparents. Except for the orderlies, who wore green overalls. One of them approached him.

'Looking for someone?'

'Yes. Mr Pappas. Room 207.'

'That way.'

Rik hurried down a well-lit corridor. The pale-pink walls were decorated with framed photographs of pets. Were the pictures to substitute for the animals that residents weren't allowed to keep? Despite the heat outside, the building smelt antiseptic, oppressively clean. Rik pressed the buzzer on the door of room 207. The door opened automatically on to a crowded room.

'You must be Rik.' The speaker wore wire-rimmed spectacles with lenses as thick as a finger. Above them were bushy black eyebrows. He looked about seventy, maybe older.

'Pleased to meet you,' Rik said, reaching out his hand. 'What should I call you?'

'I'm Niles.' He held out his hand. Rik had to lean down to shake it, for the old man was in an electric wheelchair.

'What do you think of my little empire?' Niles asked.

Rik looked around. The room was a combination of Rik's flat and his office. There was computer equipment everywhere, with several monitors, at least four hard drives and some seriously high-quality surveillance equipment. Shoved in the corner of the room, surrounded by books and magazines, was a single bed.

'Awesome!' Rik said. 'How did you get hold of all this stuff?'

'Mail order, mostly. I assemble it myself.'

'I'm impressed that you've managed to stay in the game this long given your . . . um, disability. That chair's for real, yeah?'

'A cycling accident when I was a teenager. But it didn't stop me having a family or a good career. Or playing this game. In fact, until now, the wheelchair's turned out to be very handy in hunting my targets. Easy to get around. Lots of places to hide weapons. And people tend not to suspect a cripple.'

'Must be hard to get away from your assassins, though.'

'Not really. I can't be sprayed in the complex. It's only when I leave that I'm in danger. And I only leave when I'm on a job. Also, I have lots of help. Plenty of people here without much else to do.'

'Good point,' Rik said.

'But Zorro is a nuisance. He's been my assassin for five days. He got a job here, perfectly legitimately, so I can't have him thrown out. But he always seems to be around. I want to get on and spray my new target, but each time I've tried to leave, he's been outside. My friends have tried all kinds of distraction techniques. No joy.'

'But now you've found his assassin.'

'Indeed. How many kills do you have?'

'Three. You?'

'Four. I've had a good run. I never expected to win. But maybe I can help the eventual winner.'

Rik and Niles exchanged a complicit look. 'You mean you'd . . .?'

'Yes,' Niles said. 'I'm willing to act as bait.'

THIRD MONDAY 5.15 P.M.
– SHELL

Joe and Shell had lectures that finished at five. They met Maiko afterwards and drove over to collect Mac. He was waiting in the men's changing room of a city sports centre. He'd had a shower and his blond hair was mussed, fresh smelling in the dry, dusty heat.

Shell was at the wheel of Joe's car. According to his firm's website, Badmonkey's office closed at five-thirty. However, there was no guarantee that he would leave then. The boss could go home whenever he wanted to.

The traffic was heavy and Shell wasn't used to driving in rush hour. When she got to the office block, it was nearly quarter to six. The streets were so busy, it would be easy to miss the target.

'Why are you so sure he leaves by foot?' Joe asked Mac. 'If it was me, and I was the boss, I'd use a chauffeur-driven car.'

'Arrogance? He wants to prove he can do his job, walk around like a free man and make his kills. Hold on, I think that's him!'

A man in a 'mop top' wig was leaving the office by foot. He melted into the crowd of commuters on the pavement.

'There!' Mac pointed out. 'Five paces behind him. Those are his bodyguards.'

'And where's the woman you told us about?' Shell asked from the driver's seat.

'I don't see her, but she was small,' Mac said. 'She's probably nearby.'

'OK,' Joe said. 'Let's stick to the plan. Maiko and I take out the bodyguards. Shell stays in the car and distracts the woman, if necessary, but mainly she keeps an eye out for the chick on the bike.'

Badmonkey was nearly at the end of the block now. He was waiting for the lights to change. Shell drove past him. There was no need for her to pull over to the kerb. That would draw attention to herself. The traffic was backed up, so they were stationary most of the time. That was often the way in the city. At rush hour, a pedestrian could easily outpace a driver.

Joe and Maiko got out of the car first. Mac, keeping his head down, followed them. This could all be over in seconds, Shell thought. She kept checking her rear-view mirror. No sign of a bike assassin. On the path beside her, commuters kept coming. She couldn't see Mac or the others amongst them.

The traffic started up again and the car behind her hooted. Shell had to move on. Once she got to the next block, the plan was for her to turn into a side street and wait for them. But the traffic was moving slowly. The spraying might be over before she made it to them. She looked in her rear-view mirror again. Nothing. She couldn't see Joe, Maiko or Mac. It gave her a bad feeling.

THIRD MONDAY 5.29 P.M. – RIK

The hours dragged. There had been no sign of Zorro all afternoon, but Niles said not to worry. The care orderlies' shifts were about to change. Rik sat next to Niles in the activities room, playing chess. If anyone asked, Rik was Niles's nephew.

'You're not half bad at this game,' Niles told Rik. 'If you ever fancy a rematch when all this is over, you know where to find me.'

'I might just do that,' Rik said.

'Handsome boy your age, I expect you have several women on the go, keeping you busy. That's what I was like at twenty.'

'There's just the one,' Rik said, taking a pawn.

'Tell me about her.'

Rik told the old man how he'd met Jen, how she wasn't his girlfriend, but he wanted her to be. He explained how her ex was his assassin and that he was worried that Lol would get back with Jen.

'Do you think I should invite her over here?' he asked Niles.

'Of course you should. This is only a game, Rik. If she betrays you, then at least you know you tried. If she helps you, maybe you have a partner for life. There's nothing more valuable.'

An orderly came in, pushing a drinks trolley. Rik tensed up. His hand rushed to the water pistol in his pocket. It had a short effective range, but there was also a primed super-soaker beneath the seat of Niles's wheelchair. A water weapon for any circumstance.

The orderly turned out not to be Zorro. He was too old and overweight to be the target in disguise.

'When did you last see your assassin?' Rik asked Niles.

'Two days ago. He was helping my next-door neighbour to the toilet. He winked at me. He knows that I know.'

'Still with the moustache and the pony tail?'

'Oh yes.'

'Strange that he should let you see him.'

'I've been reading up on past tournaments,' Niles said. 'By this stage of the game, players usually know who their assassin is. It tends to slow things down. You discovered who your assassin was when Jen betrayed him. Whereas, with Zorro, it's like he wants to taunt me. It would give me great pleasure were you to see him off.'

THIRD MONDAY 5.32 P.M.
– SHELL

Two minutes after Shell pulled over, Mac, Joe and Maiko were back in the car.

'Did you get him?' Shell asked, though the look on their faces told her all she needed to know.

'It wasn't Badmonkey,' Mac said. 'He looked right from a distance, but that was because of the black wig and the bodyguards behind. As soon as I sprayed him, I knew it was wrong. He was a decoy.'

'So the real Badmonkey is off attacking his own target?'

'And he's on to our method of attack,' Joe pointed out.

They drove in silence for a while, inching their way through the still heavy traffic.

'I think we should go and check out his home,' Maiko said.

'Let's get some dinner first,' Joe suggested.

'I'm not going back to the university,' Mac said. 'Too risky.'

'Your assassin's as likely to be at your flat,' Shell said.

'I've not been there for a week. Maybe I ought to check in. The assassin won't expect me to turn up there.'

'I'm hungry!' Maiko complained.

'I'll drop you two off first,' Shell offered, 'then take Mac.

That's if it's OK for me to use the car, Joe?'

Joe nodded. Shell dropped him and Maiko just outside the hall of residence. No sign of the assassin, waiting. Mac gave her directions for the last couple of streets before his flat. They pulled up in one of the shabbiest parts of town. It wasn't far from where Shell had hunted Han, before she was eliminated from the game. She stopped right outside.

'Looks clear,' Mac said.

Shell turned to him. 'Shall I come in with you?'

'There's no need.'

'Suppose Han does come by? You'll be trapped in there. And if you haven't been in for a week, you're going to need supplies. I can get them for you.'

'It's OK,' Mac said. 'Really.'

'I know what blokes are like,' Shell said. 'Don't worry. However messy it is, the place can't be worse than what I'm imagining.'

'It's not that,' Mac said.

'Give me the keys,' Shell said. 'I can make sure it's clear before you get out.'

'OK.' Mac appeared embarrassed as he handed Shell the keys. She looked up and down the street. Nobody about. She opened the outer door and walked up to Mac's first-floor flat. Again, it was quiet. She could have gone back for Mac at once, but something made her unlock the door first. She wanted to see what it was like without Mac there to monitor her reaction.

Shell wasn't sure what kind of mangy fleapit she expected to see, but it was nothing like what she found. Mac, she realized at once, had been deceiving her. He had been deceiving them all.

THIRD MONDAY 5.45 P.M. – RIK

'Checkmate in three,' Niles said, then showed Rik the combination of moves that meant he was bound to lose. 'Is that your friend?'

Jen walked across the room, looking prettier than ever. She appeared to be alone.

'What are you doing out in the open?' she asked Rik. 'Won't Zorro recognize you?'

'Doesn't matter if he does, long as I get to him first.'

'Too risky,' she said.

'We do have a plan,' Niles told her. 'Your friend here was waiting for you to arrive.'

'What's the word on Lol?' Rik asked. 'Did he follow you?'

'As if he'd tell me. But I overheard him talking to some of his mates. I think they're going to lie in wait for you at the university.'

'Great. So I won't be able to go home tonight.'

'True. But Lol doesn't know I'm seeing you, so you should be safe with me. I had a word with my mum before I borrowed her car. She says you can have our spare room for the last few days of the game. Is that OK?'

'OK? That's brilliant!'

'Good. Look, I had to explain why I was so keen on you,

but I was too embarrassed to explain how I tried to trick you for Lol – it makes me sound like such a bitch and I'm not, not really.'

'Of course you're not,' Rik said. 'What did you tell her?'

'I told her that you were my new boyfriend. I hope that's OK.'

'Fine,' Rik said, hoping that his face hadn't gone red. 'Have a seat. Niles is going to explain our plan.'

THIRD MONDAY 5.36 P.M.
– SHELL

From the outside, Mac's flat looked shabby and squalid. Inside, it was a palace, filled with pricey toys. It had shiny floorboards, an expensive stereo, handmade blinds and a state-of-the-art kitchen area. It must cost a fortune to rent, or an unimaginable amount to own. Shell looked at the leather sofa, the framed paintings on the wall. The TV alone would have taken all of her spending money for the year. How could such a young guy afford a place like this?

There were footsteps on the stairwell. She span around. Mac had followed her in.

'I got fed up of waiting,' he said. 'Street was clear.'

'How come somebody who works in a burger bar lives in a place like this?' Shell asked.

'Right question,' Mac said. 'Wrong way round. The question you should have asked was: How come someone who lives like this was working in a burger bar? I got the job because, to enter the game, you had to live and work in the area where the game was played. So I rented this place and found a job.'

'Why aren't you at college, or school, or something?'

'I'm rich,' Mac said, with a trace of an apology.

'How come? You're from a rich family?'

'Yes. I'm the only son. Dad's dead. I inherit everything.'

'Nice,' Shell said, though she wasn't sure if it was. Did Mac have a sister who didn't inherit anything?

'So Maiko, Joe and me have been taking time out of our lives to help a poor little rich boy who can afford to buy anything he wants.'

'I can't pay people to help me,' Mac told her. 'If I'm going to win, I have to win fair and square, otherwise it's meaningless. You guys helped me because you like me, and because you got thrown out of the game early on, and you missed the thrill. Isn't that true?'

Shell didn't know how to reply. She'd helped Mac for the thrill of it, sure, but mainly because she fancied him. As for the others, she didn't know. It was even harder to understand other people's motivations than it was to understand your own.

'To be honest,' she said, 'I don't know what I was thinking. But you don't need my help any more today. I'm off.'

'Wait!' Mac said. 'You seem offended. But I never actually lied to you. I'm just playing a game. I really like you, Shell. I thought you'd be pleased when you found out I wasn't just a waster . . .'

'Being rich doesn't stop you being a waster.'

'You know, if I lived round here, you're the sort of girl I'd want to be with. When you kissed me I wanted to . . . you know. But it wouldn't be fair, when I knew I'd be off home as soon as I was out of the game. I've only got three kills. I could be gone at any moment.'

'You can't be that interested if you'd be gone as soon as you're out of the game,' Shell said.

'I still like you,' Mac told her. 'And I still need your help. Please.'

'I'll think about it,' Shell said. She turned and hurried out of the open door, down the stairs, before Mac could see that she was crying. He wasn't from here. She had no chance with him. On the dusty street outside, she noticed a girl on a bike. Good luck to her.

THIRD MONDAY 7.22 P.M. – RIK

The evening meal in Senile's complex had been over for twenty minutes. There was still no sign of Zorro.

'Maybe he made us earlier,' Rik said.

'Made?' Niles said. 'What is this, a mafia movie?'

'I could try and sneak into the office,' Jen suggested, 'see if he's on shift tonight.'

'Whether he's on shift or not,' Niles told them, 'he'll want a kill. Look!'

His computer screen was open at the game's website. It showed a new leader, claiming a total of seven kills: a player who called himself Badmonkey.

Nobody knows what Badmonkey looks like, his last target had written. *All I saw was a cheap wig, probably plastic, that made him look like a member of a historical singing group. He had the most powerful water weapon I have ever come across. I was at the far side of the cinema. I thought I was safe, surrounded by friends. Yet, in the moment that the lights went down, my spraying days ended. At least I lost to a worthy adversary. I congratulate you, Badmonkey!*

'Badmonkey?' Jen said. 'What kind of a stupid name is that?'

'Never mind,' Niles said. 'Jen, I want you to book me a

taxi, one of the big limousine-type ones with a special lift for wheelchairs.'

'Where are you going?' Jen asked.

'Nowhere.'

THIRD MONDAY 7.49 P.M – HAN

Han's target was home. During the two weeks Han had been squatting in the flat, her brother had only been two streets away. Why, with all his money, did he choose to live somewhere so grotty? Han hid in a doorway that was within spraying range of Chris's doorway but not visible from his upstairs window. She'd seen his girlfriend leave two hours before. There had been no movement since. She had him cornered at last.

Tomorrow was the meeting with the Head. Han was meant to be home tonight. Suppose she rang Mum and told her what she was doing? How would Mum react? Chris had hurt her just as much as he had hurt Han. But if Han got caught, Mum might lose her daughter as well as her son. She'd probably tell Han to leave well enough alone.

A dog barked. Impatient, Han primed her super-soaker again. She wanted the maximum possible range. The flat had no rear entry. Nor was there a window at the back that Chris could jump out of. There was no fire escape at the back – she'd checked – so escaping that way wasn't an option. He would have to . . .

Why hadn't she thought of that before? The city had been on a high fire alert for weeks now. It hadn't rained once during the course of the game. With the heatwave, and the water shortage, house fires spread quickly. And nobody would risk their life for a stupid game, no matter how keen they were to win it.

There was a warehouse downtown that sold the kind of thing she needed. Han hoped that it stayed open late.

THIRD MONDAY 8.11 P.M. – RIK

Many of the complex's residents had already gone to bed. Rik waited in the empty kitchen. His target wouldn't be expecting an attack from here. Zorro might be under the impression that the whole complex counted as his workplace, so he was safe. Rik had been concerned by this. That was why he'd emailed the gamekeeper. If somebody got a new job during the course of the game, he'd asked, was their new workplace an exclusion zone? He'd got an immediate reply: no. So, if Rik saw Zorro, he could spray him.

Rik felt his phone vibrate. A text from Jen. THE TAXI'S ARRIVING. Time to get into position. He pushed open the kitchen's emergency exit and looked around. All clear. He was in the shadowy loading area. Zorro wouldn't wait here. From this side of the complex, you could see the entrance, where Senile's taxi was waiting, but it was impossible to get a shot at it. There were two places where Zorro might shoot from. A narrow upstairs window. It had been locked when Rik tried it earlier, but the assassin might have a key. More likely, he would shoot from the smoking area, to the right of the entrance. There were always one or two people hanging out there. It was within range of the area where taxis waited. And it was within range of where Rik was standing now. Just.

Niles had to make his way to the taxi alone. If Jen escorted him, Zorro might suspect that she was his assassin and use avoidance tactics. They wanted Zorro to think that Senile thought he wasn't around, so it was safe to go outside. Trouble was, Zorro might really be away. Otherwise, where had he been hiding all evening?

The doors to the main entrance opened. The taxi driver already had his ramp down. If this was to look convincing, Niles had to move into the taxi quickly. Rik watched everything on the round circular mirror that was mounted on the wall beside him. The mirror was there so that delivery vans exiting the loading bay didn't scrape a car on their way out. The view wasn't perfect but it was good enough. In a few paces, Rik could step out into full view of the entrance. He gave his super-soaker two more pumps, to maximize the pressure.

Rik's plan was to spray Zorro just as he was taking the target laminate from Niles. But when he turned the corner, things weren't going according to the plan. The wheelchair was already on the ramp. Once Niles was sealed inside the car, he was safe. Where was the assassin? Did Zorro suspect a trap? If so, he might wait for his target to return. But that didn't add up. What if Senile didn't return? What if he was escaping somewhere else and this would be Zorro's last chance to spray him? No, Zorro couldn't take that chance. So why hadn't he come out?

If Rik were Zorro, what would he do? In the taxi's mirror, Rik saw Niles gave an anxious glance in his direction. He hadn't been sprayed. His sacrifice had been pointless. Unless . . . suddenly, Rik worked out what he would do in Zorro's situation. He only had a few seconds. The wheelchair was about to lock into place. Once that happened, the taxi door would automatically close and . . . Rik ran out of the parking bay, into the entrance area, not caring who saw him.

'Stop!' he shouted to Niles. 'Don't let him close the door!'

Too late. The door slid automatically across. Niles gave Rik a bewildered stare. The taxi didn't move though. The driver smiled at Rik, then turned to his sole passenger, a compact water pistol in his hand. Senile's sacrifice was for nothing. Zorro soaked him, then took his laminate.

Rik watched as Zorro closed the glass partition between driver and passenger, then unloaded the wheelchair. The damp, disabled man steered himself back into the complex. Zorro gave Rik a regal wave as he drove off. Now he knew who his assassin was. Rik's small advantage was gone.

'He outsmarted us,' Niles told Rik in his most philosophical voice. 'Ah well, you knew he was good.'

'It was worth a try,' Jen said. She gave Niles a hug then turned to Rik. 'Come on, I'll drive you home.'

'Wait,' Rik said. 'Niles, do you mind telling me who your next target was to be? It's my best way of getting to Zorro.'

It's a tough one,' Niles said. 'A young girl. She's never where she's meant to be and I only caught a fleeting glimpse of her once, riding a bike. She calls herself Han.'

THIRD TUESDAY 12.14 A.M.
– MAC

Mac was tempted to book a hotel room for the night. It would be safer than going home, or staying with Shell and Joe, even presuming they were OK about him misleading them. He'd not lied. He had never claimed to be poor. People assumed Mac was skint because he worked in a burger bar. So he acted skint. Slumming it was part of the experience of the game. That was why he was reluctant to stay in a hotel tonight, even though he could afford the best in town.

He didn't feel like going back to his flat though. Shell had soured it for him. And there might be an assassin waiting outside.

You could take slumming it too far. Living in a rough part of town was one thing, but Mac needed a comfortable flat for the rare occasions that he was there – after all, he might be trapped inside it for ages. The place he was renting was so flash, Mac reckoned it belonged to a criminal of some kind. It had state-of-the-art video, high-speed Internet, air conditioning to keep out the torrid summer heat.

Mac had only spent a couple of nights in the flat since the game began. He had slept on Ben's sofa and the floor of Joe's room. Any discomfort was well worth it for the advantage it gave him in the game. He'd made it to the final week of the game on his third attempt. Now he had his toughest target yet. Badmonkey must have been out tonight, for Mac had waited by his smart apartment all evening, carefully concealed between two parked cars.

Maybe he should buy himself a car for the last week of the game. Mac didn't have a licence in this country, or, indeed, in any country, but he could drive. He hadn't got around to taking his test yet, that was the only problem. At this stage, it was probably cheaper and easier to use taxis, as he was doing now.

'Which house is it, mate?'

'Just go round the corner.'

Another reason Mac suspected that his flat's owner was crooked was that it had a useful, secret escape route. You'd never have guessed, but the building had a fire door on the second floor. This led to a narrow passageway linking four houses on the street, with an exit in the corner house, which had an old-fashioned iron fire escape. Mac wouldn't want to use it often as a way in, or out. If he did, it wouldn't stay secret for long. But it certainly came in handy at times when he was likely to be watched, like now.

'Sorry,' the driver said. 'Can't get down this road. Looks like there's something going on.'

Mac swore. 'Just go round the other way, would you?'

'Don't think I can. It's the emergency services, see? They're connected to the water main. They're blocking the next street, too.'

'Can you get a bit closer?' Mac didn't want to get out of

the car, but he was getting an uncomfortable feeling.

'Too dangerous, mate. See that smoke? I think it's a fire.'

'Wait there. I'll be right back.'

'Fare first, please.'

'I'm leaving my bag,' Mac said. 'I'll be right back.'

'No offence, but I've had people pull tricks on me before. You know how it is, they leave a bag full of rubbish and—'

Mac handed him a large note. 'I'll be back. Wait there.'

He hurried round the corner. There were two fire engines on his street. He turned to one of the fire fighters.

'Was anybody hurt?'

'Too soon to say. We've only just arrived. Do you live here?'

'Yes. First floor. Any idea how bad the damage is?'

'Not yet. But you'll need to find somewhere else to stay tonight.'

THIRD TUESDAY 10.27 A.M. – RIK

Jen's home was just inside the city limits, but felt like it belonged to a different world. Inside, the house was airy and comfortable. It had running water, so Rik was able to have a shower when he got up. Jen didn't have a lesson until eleven-fifteen, so she shared a late breakfast with Rik. Her mother cooked eggs, acting as chaperone. She kept asking Rik questions: Why wasn't he at university himself? How many serious girlfriends had he had before? Rik ducked them as best he could. He didn't need to go to university. With his skills, he could get a job anywhere. He could follow Jen anywhere, if she were really his girlfriend – but he didn't say this out loud.

The texts started to flood in at ten-thirty, which was morning break. At first, Jen ignored them, busy eating her eggs. Then she got one that drew her attention.

'It's Lol,' she said. 'I'd better see what he wants. If he finds out you're staying here, we could be in trouble.' She opened the text. 'Oh my . . .' her eyes widened and she passed the phone to Rik.

'What is it?' her mum said.

'Lol got sprayed last night. He wanted to know if his assassin has sprayed Rik already. Evidently, he's really good.'

Rik passed the phone back. Jen went through her other messages. 'I don't believe this!' she told him. 'Now there are only five players left. You've made it to the last five! That's incredible.'

'It's not bad,' Rik said, 'but I have to spray Zorro and avoid being sprayed by . . . can we check the game website? I should be able to work out who my assassin is.'

'We've got five minutes,' Jen said. 'I'll just boot my laptop up.'

'Or you could look out of the window,' Jen's mum told them. 'There's a man in a three-piece suit and a Beatles wig getting out of a limousine. Do you think by any chance that could be him?'

THIRD TUESDAY 10.30 A.M.
– SHELL

'Don't think that because I let you stay here last night, we're a team again,' Shell told Mac. 'If someone hadn't set fire to your place . . .'

'We don't know that's what happened. It may have been a coincidence.'

'Crap. She was trying to smoke you out. Did you report it to the gamekeeper?'

'I emailed him before I went to sleep. I got a reply while you were making breakfast. He's investigating.'

'So you won't go back to your flat?' Shell said, not sure if she wanted him to stay or not. If something was going to happen between her and Mac, it would have happened by now.

'No, but I can get a hotel tonight.'

'I think that's for the best.'

'But I still need your help.'

'Why should I give it?' Shell asked, starting to soften.

'Because we're friends?'

'Friends don't keep big secrets from each other.'

'I don't understand why you're annoyed about that. Most girls I've met are pretty happy that I'm rich.'

'I'm not most girls,' Shell said. 'I thought we were friends but you held back a big thing about yourself, that's what annoys me. Why would I be impressed, just because you've inherited money?'

'I'm not saying you should be. It's just . . . since my dad died, I don't need to work. I've got nothing going on except this game. And right here, right now, you're the closest friend I've got.'

Shell felt a little bit sorry for him. If she was honest with herself, Mac hadn't encouraged her, except as a friend. Nor had he lied to her, not exactly. She was angry because he had hidden part of his life from her. But maybe that was his right. It was a game, after all.

Shell chose her next words carefully.

'OK. I'll help you to try and find Badmonkey. I've come this far, I'd like to see how the game ends. Have you looked at the website this morning? According to the betting, he and Zorro are joint favourites.'

'Really? Where do I rank in the betting?'

'Third.'

'With you on my side,' Mac promised. 'I'll do better than that.'

THIRD TUESDAY 10.38 A.M. – RIK

Jen's mum drove her to school, leaving Rik behind. He was trapped in his girlfriend's house. If she *was* his girlfriend. Rik could have gone with Jen, but didn't want his assassin to know that he was here. He should have known that Lol would shop him to whoever his new assassin was. The guy outside was either Mac or Badmonkey. Both were very dangerous. The Beatles wig suggested that it was Badmonkey, but the assassin could be playing a double bluff.

How far away was Jen's school? Rik needed to get after Zorro, but he didn't have a clue where to find him. A car pulled up outside.

'He's still there,' Jen's mum told Rik, 'lingering behind the carport. Does he think you're stupid enough to come out?'

'I was rather hoping you'd drive me somewhere,' Rik said.

'He'd spray you before you got in the car, I'm afraid. I expect we can find a way to get rid of him. I could call the police, for instance. Or is that outside the rules of the game?'

'I don't think the police would be too happy. They'd say he's here because I choose to play the game. Sorry. Also, I could do without running into them again because . . .' He told her about the scam he'd pulled in the central police station.

'That was before you met Jen, wasn't it? How exactly did you meet Jen? I know she tried to register for the game but didn't get in.'

'Um . . .' Rik didn't want to lie, but he didn't want to drop Jen in it, either, by letting on how she'd been doing Lol's dirty work. He decided to be circumspect. 'We bumped into each other on a bus.'

Outside, Badmonkey lay in wait, not even bothering to hide.

THIRD TUESDAY 9.14 A.M. – ZED

'At least I got taken out by the top player,' Zed said.

She was looking over Yogi's shoulder as he read the game website. The odds listed were based on each players' kill results and bets being taken. Badmonkey and Zorro were joint favourites. Next came Mac, then Rik, then, finally, Han. There were no other players left in the game.

'It seems so long ago that we were both in it,' Yogi said. 'We were willing to hide out in that container for three weeks. Can you imagine if we were still there?'

'I can't see us still being a couple if we were,' Zed said. 'That place was seriously claustrophobic.'

The doorbell rang.

'Expecting someone?' Zed asked.

'An informant.'

'Here?' At our home?'

'Believe me, this is an informant you'll want to meet.'

Zed opened the door to a good-looking guy of about her own age. His hair was short and he had a small cleft in his chin, which she'd read somewhere denoted selfishness. He gave her a thin smile and said hello in an accent that she couldn't place.

'You look familiar,' she said. 'Have we met before?'

'Yes, but I was wearing a mac and silly glasses.'

'Wow!' she said. 'You're the gamekeeper.'

'I am. Is Yogi here?'

'Come in, come in.'

Zed got the gamekeeper some water while he introduced himself to Yogi.

'Have you any way of proving that you're you?' her boyfriend asked. 'I mean, I met one of your assistants and assumed he was you.'

'It doesn't really matter who I am,' the gamekeeper said. 'This game's been going on for years. I'm not the first gamekeeper and I won't be the last. All of us like to keep our identities secret, to avoid legal difficulties and press interest. So far, over the many years that the game has been played, there have been no serious problems. A few minor injuries, that's all.'

'So far?'

'I've come to see you because your entry details show that you're a police officer. Is that correct?'

'It is. You want to see me in an official capacity?'

'I thought it best to come to an officer who I know is friendly to the game. Of course, I understand that you will have to pass on the information I give you. But first, I hope to get your advice.'

'Shoot,' Yogi said.

'One of our leading players emailed me in the early hours of this morning. He thinks his home was firebombed in an attempt to drive him outside, where his assassin could spray him.'

'Ouch,' said Zed. 'Was anybody hurt?'

'Luckily not. And the target wasn't home. I may be overreacting, but I have tried to contact the assassin concerned, who calls herself Han. Unfortunately, all of her details are fake.'

'Don't you check people out before they start the game?'

'We meet them all in person. My assistant was a little concerned that she might be underage, which would disqualify her from winning but is hardly a matter of great concern.'

'Do you have a photo?'

The gamekeeper handed Yogi a target laminate. 'It's not very good. There's too much hair. You can barely make out her face.'

'Have you contacted her?'

'I emailed her early this morning and asked her to meet me. So far, there's been no response.'

'And which player did she try to firebomb?'

'The one who calls himself Mac.'

'He's the guy who sprayed me.'

'He's a strong player. It appears she thought he was home, but he had a secret exit from the flat where he was staying and had left before she started the fire.'

'How bad was it?'

'He doesn't know yet. I was hoping that you could find out.'

Yogi thought for a moment. 'I need to take this to my boss. I'm not on shift until this afternoon. Do you know who's in charge of the arson investigation?'

'Afraid not.'

'Any means of getting in touch with this Mac character?'

'I can give you his mobile phone number. He doesn't have an address, for obvious reasons.'

'OK. I'll need that, along with your full name and address. This isn't just a game any more.'

The gamekeeper winced when Yogi came out with this cliché, but gave him the information he needed. Then he programmed Yogi's number into his mobile and promised to phone if the girl who called herself Han got in touch.

'It might be best if the game finished very quickly, before anybody gets seriously hurt,' Yogi told him.

'Point taken,' the gamekeeper said. 'But I might be overreacting. The fire could have been a coincidence. There have been a lot of fires in the city lately.'

THIRD TUESDAY 2.11 P.M. – HAN

Han knew she'd screwed up as soon as the fire alarm went off and she saw people running from the other end of the street. Her brother was always cunning. How was she supposed to work out that his flat had a fire escape three doors away? She'd never been inside. She'd cycled straight over to the fire escape, but everyone was already out. Either Chris escaped then or, more likely, he'd sneaked out much earlier and was stalking his victim while she waited to spray him.

The smoke bombs caused rather more panic than she'd meant to happen. Some damage, too. She felt bad about smoking everybody out. It seemed like a good idea at the time. Luckily, nobody got hurt when they hurried from their homes. But it had been a stupid, risky thing to do. The police were unlikely to catch her. Even if Han had been CCTVed, she was wearing a bike helmet and face mask. Only Chris would know that she was responsible. And Chris was an honourable player. He'd never grass her up to the police.

But he had given her up to the gamekeeper. This morning, before school, she'd opened an email from him.

I have received reports that you have been setting fires to flush your target from his home. This is against the spirit and rules of the Spray game. In addition, two of your previous targets have complained that you are too young to be part of this game and must have faked your ID. My assistant says that he had his doubts about your age when you were handed your laminate and noted this at the time.

I am, therefore, suspending you from the Spray game. You have until six p.m. tonight to answer these charges to my satisfaction. Otherwise, you will be eliminated from the game.

Han hadn't replied. A smoke bomb wasn't the same as starting a fire. It was hardly dangerous at all. But she had no way to deflect the accusation of being underage. She was out. So be it. Her aim had always been to get Chris. Beating him in the game would have been a bonus. But it wasn't her main priority.

She had a more pressing problem to deal with. A buzzer sounded and she stood up.

'You can come in now,' the Head said, holding her office door open. 'Your mother and I have finished talking.'

Framed photos of school alumni covered the pale-pink walls. Han sat down in a black leather chair with a stiff back. The Head was younger than her mother, and fiercer.

'I know you've had a difficult three years,' the Head said. 'The divorce, your mother's remarriage, then your father's death and your brother's disappearance. But you are reaching a crucial point in your school career. Your exam courses are under way. Mistakes you make now could haunt you for the rest of your life. Skipping school is never wise. And there is no excuse for dishonesty. None at all.'

Han put on a serious face. 'It's not as bad as you think,' she said. 'I've not been with a boy, or on drugs, or anything like that.'

'Then where have you been?' Mum asked.

'You know how, the other day, you were on about how Chris used to chase me round with a water pistol when we were kids?'

'Yes,' Mum said. The Head looked bemused. 'Wasn't there something on the TV—'

'And how he kept a scrapbook about the Water War game that travels from city to city?'

'I've read about that,' the Head said. 'It was a craze at school, for a while.'

'The thing is, the game's been on in the city, here, for the last two and a half weeks. So I had to play. That's where I've been, hiding in the city, sneaking up on people with a water pistol. I made it into the final week. But I've been eliminated now. It's all over. I'm sorry about the deception, really. But I'm done. I won't do anything like this again. I'm sorry.'

'Well,' the Head said. 'That is a relief. I do think that this is the sort of matter that ought to be dealt with in the home, rather than at school. So I suggest that you get back to your lessons, make up for the work missed, and we'll say no more about it.'

'That's very generous of you,' Mum said. 'Thank you so much for your time.'

They left the office. Han was about to head towards the last lesson of the day when Mum grabbed her by the shoulder.

'Have you seen him?' she asked. 'Did you see your brother?'

THIRD TUESDAY 4.14 P.M. – RIK

Jen got home from school to find Rik reading a newspaper. Her mum had left for work, taking the car with her. Rik risked kissing Jen on the cheek. If he acted like her boyfriend, maybe he would become that person.

'Any sign of my assassin?' he asked.

'I think he's gone,' Jen said. 'But best not to risk it.'

'I'm meant to be at work later tonight.'

'I'll pinch Mum's car when she gets back from work and take you there if you want.'

'If you could get my shift patterns, I'll bet Badmonkey can too.'

'Don't forget, he's being hunted. He'll have to be careful.'

'You're right,' Rik said. 'I've been trawling the website and chat boards, trying to work out who's hunting who. There are five players left and, assuming nobody's been reassigned, Zorro can't be Badmonkey's assassin, so it must be Han or Mac. Trouble is, they're the two players I haven't come across yet. So I wouldn't recognize either of them.'

'Is there a way for you to contact one of them and tell them where Badmonkey is?'

'Maybe. But as soon as they've sprayed Badmonkey they could spray me.'

Jen thought for a minute. 'You could leave telling them until there are just three players left, then drop Badmonkey in it and spray his assassin before he or she has time to take the laminate.'

'You've got just the kind of devious mind that I like,' Rik said.

'I'll take that as a major compliment,' Jen said, and kissed him lightly on the lips.

THIRD WEDNESDAY 10.31 A.M.
– MAC

Stalemate. Mac had spent all night outside Badmonkey's house, but the businessman had not come home. There was no sign of him near the office either. He got a taxi back to Shell's, where he checked the game website. One more player was down. That left him, his assassin, his target, a guy called Rik and the favourite, Zorro.

Mac hadn't been back to his flat, but he had spoken to the fire department. Turned out there was no fire.

'Some joker set off three smoke bombs in the entrance hall. We covered it in foam before we realized there was no danger. Most people have gone back to their flats now, but there'll be a bit of a smell. And you're probably better off going in the back way. The entrance hall's in a right mess.'

So Mac's assassin, whoever she was, was responsible. But she hadn't put anyone's life in danger. Immediately after this call, Mac had phoned the gamekeeper on the number he'd given him.

'Yes, my police contact told me the same thing. But I've suspended your assassin from the game anyway.'

'So I don't have an assassin at the moment?'

'Keep your phone switched on. And be warned, you won't get a free run for long.'

Now Mac's mobile vibrated against his chest. Could this be his assassin, taunting him? No, it was the gamekeeper, who Mac had contacted the day before. He had news.

'The girl who calls herself Han hasn't responded to my emails, which suggests that she did set off the smoke bombs at your flat. I have, reluctantly at this late stage, eliminated her from the game.'

'For a few smoke bombs?'

'No. The email I sent noted that two of her victims have complained that she is underage.'

Mac was curious about Han. He kept trying to imagine what she looked like beneath her face mask. She didn't look that young to him. There was something about her, something familiar and foxy. He'd half hoped she would be his final opponent. The smoke bomb was a smart move. If he'd been in, she might well have got him.

'She didn't look underage to me,' he said.

'She's failed to furnish proof that she's sixteen,' the gamekeeper said. 'There are legal reasons why we insist on the age thing.'

'Does that mean that you've reinstated her last target, DC?'

'Wouldn't work. If we did that, I'd have to reinstate all of Han's victims back to the start of the game. My only choice was to make her assassin your assassin. I'm about to inform him of the change.'

'Him?'

'All four of the players left in the game are male. You can

probably work out which one is your new assassin.'

Mac thought for a moment. It couldn't be Badmonkey. That left a guy called Rik or . . .

'I'm being pursued by Zorro?'

'I thought it fair to warn you. Good luck.'

THIRD WEDNESDAY 4.52 P.M. – HAN

School was a shock to the system. Han had no time to sneak off and check her webmail account. When she got home, it was no surprise to find an email from the gamekeeper. He had eliminated her from the game, not for the smoke bombs, but for being underage. In a way, it was fair. Whoever won the game would get a lot of publicity. If it turned out the winner was a fifteen-year-old girl, that would undermine the game in the future. You'd get loads more underage kids trying to enter. Han wasn't bothered by being thrown out. She'd never entered the game to win. She'd entered it to get to Chris.

The email from the gamekeeper finished:

```
Do not be offended by my enforcement of
the rules. I hope you will still attend
the end-of-game party. You'll be sent an
invitation to the secret venue. This
will be posted to your registered
address, unless you prefer it to be sent
elsewhere, in which case please inform
me of the new address by Thursday
morning at the latest.
```

Was this a ploy to get her real address or did he actually want her at the party? It hardly mattered. Han wasn't interested in partying with water game players or meeting the gamekeeper. She was only interested in finding Chris. Not at a party with loads of other people, but on her own, face to face. Was that too much to ask?

She checked the game website. Things had gone quiet. No kills reported in more than forty-eight hours. The last four players were being cagey, as well they might. Each was so close to victory. The gamekeeper would have to speed things up if they were going to finish by Sunday. In previous games, he had made himself a target. It would be good if he did so again. She needed a situation that brought her brother out into the open.

THIRD WEDNESDAY 10.38 P.M.
– SHELL

'Thanks for coming,' Mac told Shell, as she joined him in a quiet corner of the bar. Earlier, she'd offered him a room in hall for another night, but he was worried about Zorro tracking him down there, and refused. Halls were vulnerable places, as Rik and Zorro had proved on the first night of the game. Half an hour ago, he'd phoned to say that he was lonely, and was sending a car to pick her up. Against her better judgement, she'd agreed to visit his temporary home, a plush place on the edge of the business district.

'Nice hotel,' she said.

'Hotels are boring. I'd rather be out hunting Badmonkey, but his home security's superb. My only chance of getting him is if I catch him trying to spray Rik, and I can't track Rik down.'

'He works at the university,' Shell said. 'I'll bet we can find him tomorrow. But what if your assassin tracks you here?'

'I used my real name to book in, so he'd find it tricky. There are so many hotels in the city, Zorro can't scope them all. But if anyone can get me, he can.'

'You were always going to come up against him if you're going to win,' Shell pointed out.

'It won't be the first time,' Mac told her.

'No?'

'He eliminated me in London, when I played there. First week. I'd just made my first kill and was really proud of myself. I was running for a bus when, suddenly, this guy with a moustache leant out of a passing taxi cab and sprayed me. Classic move.'

'So you've played the game before? In different cities?'

'I didn't break any rules. I got a job in the city, working as a porter. In San Francisco, I was a cleaner.'

'You've been to San Francisco? What's that like?'

'I made it to the second week. It's a fantastic city. You have to go sometime . . .'

He talked about his travels for an hour. At first, Shell was fascinated, but after a while she noted that he never once asked about her. Nor did he notice when she stopped asking questions or even nodding. Mac had quite an ego on him when he got going. Only when he went to order another beer did he see that the bar had closed.

'Want to continue the conversation in my suite?'

A week ago, Shell might have jumped at this offer.

'I don't think that's a good idea,' she said. Mac might be rich and good-looking but he was a year younger than her and, with a few drinks inside him, his lack of maturity showed. She was no longer tempted.

'You're right. I need to be sharp tomorrow.'

'Perhaps you can ask the doorman to call the car round.'

THIRD THURSDAY 11.58 A.M.
– RIK

Rik was planning his endgame. One player, Han, had been eliminated, for reasons that weren't clear. Rik was after Zorro who was after Mac who was after Badmonkey who was after him.

Rik was at work. Might as well earn some money while the game was so dead. If this stalemate lasted much longer, he knew, the gamekeeper would initiate some kind of sudden-death shoot-out.

Being big, Rik didn't move as fast as some of the other competitors. He was better suited to a tactical game than a physical one. Luckily, he had Jen to help him. Today she was skiving off school, waiting near the university, trying to track Badmonkey down. There was no point in her trying to locate the elusive Zorro. The only sensible move was to draw the two-time champion to him. Where Badmonkey was, Mac was likely to be. And where Mac was, Zorro wouldn't be far behind.

Jen had promised to call at midday and she did, on the dot.

'I found Badmonkey. He's in a chauffeur-driven car that's holed up in the vice chancellor's parking space, would you believe.'

'Any sign of Mac?'

'No. But I noticed a tall blonde keeping an eye on the car and using her mobile.'

Rik knew the girl he meant, a former player called Shell. 'Mac could be on his way. Question is, how do we alert Zorro?'

'If he's as good as you say he is, Zorro's on to it already.'

THIRD THURSDAY 12.02 P.M.
– MAC

Mac sat in the back of Joe's car, hunched up so that he couldn't be seen.

'You say this Rik guy definitely works on campus?'

'S'right,' Joe said and selected the photo he'd taken on his phone. 'He showed us his ID card when he came to Shell's room the day before the game began. That's when I took this.'

'The card could have been a fake.'

'I've seen him around. He works here. So Badmonkey will be watching him here. If Shell's right, Mr Arrogant is parked in front of the vice chancellor's office, just down the road from IT.'

'He can't spray Rik within a block of his work,' Mac reminded him.

'Rik has to walk further than a block to get his bus home. Maybe he's got a friend who'll drive him to his apartment, but there are bound to be moments when he's at risk, like when he gets out of the car. We have to hope that Rik draws Badmonkey out for us.'

'Zorro's bound to work out that this is where all the action is.'

'You should be safe if you stay in the back of the car most of the time. Nobody can spray you there.'

'But I can't spray anybody either,' Mac reflected. 'Once I open the window to spray Badmonkey, I'm vulnerable.'

Mac's phone rang again. Shell.

'Rik's on the move.'

THIRD THURSDAY 12.06 P.M.
– RIK

Rik had his super-soaker tucked in the huge right pocket of his baggy pants. He kept a tiny water pistol in his left, a red plastic thing he'd got free with a kids' comic: it had a surprisingly good range. He should be safe until he got near the bus stop. Jen would pick him up before that. Where was Badmonkey? Where was Mac? His mobile rang.

'Badmonkey's on the move,' Jen said. 'I'm following.'

'Any sign of the others?'

'Not yet. But I saw the girl getting into an old car.'

'We need to open this up,' Rik told her. 'Get everyone out of their cars.'

'Then you have to walk somewhere they can't go in a car.'

'I'll tell you what,' Rik said. 'Instead of turning right, towards the bus stop, I'll cross the road and head into the library.'

'That's not your workplace. You could get sprayed.'

'Don't worry. I've spent a lot of time in that library. I know my way around. As long as I get there safely. Where's Badmonkey now?'

'He's a couple of minutes behind you.'

'OK. Pick me up. Give me a lift to the library.'

Rik stood by the road and waited for Jen. He imagined a

big finale scene in the library, players stalking each other between the aisles. He could picture a Mexican stand-off, with all four assassins stood in a circle, each pointing their weapon at their target, but reluctant to shoot. For if they all shot at once, there could be no winner.

The whole thing was in danger of descending into farce. A librarian was bound to come along and interrupt the scene, throw them out. At which point, they would start spraying, soaking the librarian, each other and a whole lot of books. The sharpest player – Rik, hopefully – would duck behind the book stacks, keep dry, then step out to spray the already-soaked other players, and win the game.

Jen was driving down Campus Road. Ahead of her, a long, grey limo loomed into view. If Badmonkey got out and sprayed him, Rik would have a right to complain. He was only a short distance from his workplace, but people had been sprayed just outside campus buildings and the hit had been upheld by the gamekeeper. This wasn't a game you played with a calculator and a measuring tape. Thanks to turning the wrong way, he could be about to be sprayed.

Jen's car edged right up to the limo. The road was wide, but not that wide. Had Badmonkey's driver seen Rik? Yes, he was accelerating, fast. Rik looked for cover, but there was none. His assassin was bound to be quicker than he was. Running away was no good. The library plan had been a bad idea. He should have gone to the bus stop, which was nearer.

Just behind Rik, the limo screeched to a halt. Another car nearly rear-ended it, stopping just as abruptly. Next moment, Jen's car skidded around the limo, narrowly missing a bus that was coming in the opposite direction. She opened her passenger door. Rik hurried towards her, aware that his assassin was getting out of the limo. At any moment, he was likely to feel water on his back. The game would be over.

Jen's mum's car was a compact. Rik had to squeeze in. He struggled to pull the door shut before he was properly sat down.

'Is he behind me? he asked Jen.

'Oh, he's behind you all right,' Jen said. 'But you've no need to worry. Look around.'

Rik twisted his head back. A middle-aged man with close-cropped hair was on the grass verge. Instead of a water pistol, the man was holding a black 'mop top' wig. The wig was sopping wet. Badmonkey was out of the game. Behind Badmonkey was a handsome guy with blond curly hair. For a moment, Rik thought that he was the gamekeeper, come to announce the conclusion of the competition. But then he saw Badmonkey hand over his laminate. The young guy was his new assassin. Mac.

Jen's car was too small for Rik to comfortably pump up the pressure on his super-soaker. He reached into his left pocket for the tiny red water pistol and scanned the horizon.

'Any sign of Zorro?' he asked Jen.

'No. Doesn't mean he isn't about to make a move. Hold on.'

She did a U-turn in the middle of the road, swinging back past the limo and the car that Mac had come in. A student who Rik recognized was in the driver's seat. He was the one who'd taken a photo of him with his phone, the day before the game started. Of Zorro, there was no sign.

'I think we'd better get out of here,' Rik told Jen.

FINAL FRIDAY 5.00 P.M. – HAN

'Do you really think Chris is in the city for the water fight game?' Mum asked Han. 'Wouldn't he have contacted us?'

'Why? It's been nearly three years,' Han said. 'As far as he's concerned, we don't exist.'

'All the more reason for him not to come here.'

'He is here,' Han said. 'I've seen him.'

'Did he see you?'

She shook her head. She could have gone for Chris in the car park, but wanted to get him alone, with no witnesses. It was too late to get him as part of the game, but she could still have her revenge.

'Why didn't you talk to him?'

'First he took away my father, then he took my inheritance. I didn't want to talk to him. I wanted to beat him, to show that I'm better than him.'

'But you didn't succeed. I'm sorry, Han.'

'I only failed because they found out I was too young to be in the game.'

'I see. The thing is, you may not want to see your brother, but I do. I owe him an apology. When I married your stepfather, I drove him away.'

'You're right, you did.' This was weird. Until this week,

she and Mum never discussed Chris. Not even at Christmas and birthdays.

'Do you think your brother's involved in this Water War thing at the city park as well as the Spray game? I just saw an item on the news. The organizers have refused to cancel it. A little childish, if you ask me, wasting all that water when there's a drought.'

'Everyone needs to be a little childish sometimes,' Han said, and left the room before Mum could come up with some smart retort.

Upstairs, she checked the game's website. She'd been waiting for an announcement about the end of the game. The details were there. The whole thing would finish tomorrow, in the park. This would be her last chance to get to Chris, unless she went to the party. Han wasn't good at parties. She preferred one-to-ones. And Chris, if he was as proud as ever, might not go to the party, not unless he won. There were only three players left, but the other two were very, very good. Han wanted to get to her brother before one of them did.

Han got out the revolver that used to belong to her stepdad. She'd been carrying around it around for days, even before she became Mac's assassin. Tomorrow would be her last chance to use it.

FINAL SATURDAY 11.24 A.M.
– MAC

Mac and Shell took a taxi from Mac's hotel to the campus, where Mac checked his mail on Joe's computer. He found an email addressed to him, Zorro and Rik. It had been sent by the gamekeeper the day before.

> But three of you remain. One will be left standing to collect the prize at the party on Sunday. To expedite matters, you are to attend the Water War at City Park on Saturday. You must stay within the park grounds from midday until you have either won or been assassinated. No spraying before two p.m. I will verify your attendance in person. Have your phone about you and turned on. You may assassinate your opponents in whatever order you choose. Good luck at the conclusion of this historic battle!

This 'final' was also announced on the game's website. It

wasn't 'sudden death', not exactly. Whether Mac sprayed Rik or Zorro first, he could still be taken out by whichever player remained. And the City Park would be full of amateurs with water weapons, so the chances of being sprayed by someone else were high. But the whole thing was fair, he saw that. The game was Mac's to win. He could be the champion by the end of the afternoon.

'You don't need us any more,' Shell said, her voice resigned.

'You're right, I'm on my own. But if I lose, I'll join you in the Water War,' Mac said. 'It'll be fun to spray people at random instead of always waiting around for half a chance to get my target.'

'You'd better register then,' Joe said. 'OK, strategy meeting!'

The rules for the Water War weren't complex. There were two teams. You were assigned to a team on arrival and given a stapled wristband that changed colour, permanently, when it got wet. If the wristband was removed or tampered with in any way, the player was eliminated from the game. The last player to avoid getting soaked was the winner. The game began at two. In previous years, when the main play was over, the Water War degenerated into a free-for-all until players got bored or – a distinct possibility this year – they ran out of water.

'Will you really get a wristband?' Shell asked Mac.

'You bet. Taking part in the Water War is the best cover I can think of.'

FINAL SATURDAY 11.58 A.M.
– RIK

Rik walked into the park with Jen at his side. They had already visited once, the evening before, and watched the preparations for the day's events. In a sudden-death shoot-out like this, his girth was a handicap. Planning was everything. He looked for the gamekeeper.

'Don't worry,' Jen said. She leant against him, reached up and kissed him full on the lips. 'You're going to win. I know it!'

'I've already won if you keep kissing me like that,' Rik said. Jen gave him a reassuring smile. Hard to believe, but she really was his girlfriend.

When they reached the middle of the park, near the lake, they stopped and waited. The gamekeeper appeared from behind a tree whose leaves were an unseasonable brown. He held out his hand.

'Congratulations on making it this far. I wanted a chance to speak to each of the players in person before the game begins. I also want to make it clear that there is to be no spraying before two p.m. A hit before then doesn't count. Understood?'

'Understood,' Rik said.

'And you're on your own. Your friend can watch. She can play in the other water game that's on here today, but she can't help you by hindering or spraying either of your targets.'

'Understood,' Rik said. 'How do we verify our kills?'

'Good question. I'll be watching from the city police security cameras.'

'They let you use security cameras?' Jen asked.

'I'm one of the sponsors of the city's annual water game. It's no coincidence that the Water War takes place this weekend. But I can't guarantee that I'll see the final fatal shots. As always, in the Spray game, we operate on mutual trust and respect. If you get sprayed, hand over your laminate and come to the security HQ by the café.'

'And if I don't?'

'Then you'll be a worthy winner.'

'Have the others arrived? Are they here yet?'

'I met Zorro a few minutes ago. He's sat at the edge of the playground, over there. Mac will be here soon. I want to introduce the three of you, go over the rules ones last time.'

Rik and Jen strolled over to the playground. Zorro sat on a bench, on his own. He had a water pack on his back, combat trousers and a khaki T-shirt. On his wrist was a tag for the Water War game. Rik had decided not to get one of those.

'We meet again,' Zorro said. 'It's been a long three weeks.'

'You're a hard man to track down,' Rik told him.

'That's how I stay alive.'

Up close, Zorro was plumper of face than Rik remembered, and older: over thirty.

'How many tournaments is this now?' he asked the veteran.

'My sixth. Won three, lost three. And my last, probably.'

'Why's that?'

'About to become a dad. Time to put aside childish things.'

'Congratulations,' Rik said, aware that Zorro was looking over his shoulder. 'Is he here?'

Zorro nodded. 'Hard to tell them apart from this distance, but I think that's Mac.'

'People are saying that he's the next you. That he travelled a long way to be in this game.'

'Getting to the last three is a good achievement,' Zorro told Rik. 'But it doesn't make Mac me. There's only one me. You, I like. You're an unusual player. Very tactical. You were the assassin I was most scared of.'

Rik noted Zorro's use of the past tense, said nothing. The gamekeeper and Mac were walking over. The two men stood. Hands were shaken. Mac said nothing to Zorro, which was probably wise. It didn't do to get too friendly with your opponents.

'You have the best part of two hours to check the lie of the land, have lunch, do whatever you want,' the gamekeeper said. 'But you must not leave the park until the game is over. If you do, you lose. Understood?'

They all mumbled that they understood.

'All right,' said the gamekeeper. 'Let the final begin!'

FINAL SATURDAY 12.15 P.M. – MAC

Mac left the other contestants and joined Shell, Joe and Maiko. All four of them queued to register for the Water War game.

'I can't believe you've come this far,' Joe told him.

'Me neither,' Mac said.

'Shell says you've played the game twice before,' Maiko said.

'That's right. Never made it to the final week though.'

'Let's hope it's third time lucky,' Shell said, and gave him a hug.

They got their wristbands and separated. Shell and Maiko were assigned red, Joe and Mac blue.

'You've all got my mobile number, yeah?' Mac said. 'In case you spot either of my rivals.'

All nodded enthusiastically.

'We'll help you if we can,' Joe told Mac, 'but remember, all three of us are in this game to win!'

'Me too,' Mac said. 'Good luck.'

They set off in search of safe cover.

FINAL SATURDAY 12.54 P.M. – RIK

Rik's best chance of winning was to hide, and surprise his enemy. The easiest place to hide, Rik reckoned, was in plain sight. This was harder for a guy his size, but not impossible. He had a plan.

The park had a café adjacent to the lake in the centre, with a gift shop and a takeaway drinks area. Just behind it was the Portakabin in which the game's security HQ was based. The café was where Rik waited for the game to begin. Jen was half a metre away, on lookout, waiting near the Water War registration table, hidden behind the living statues.

Rik had eaten a light lunch, as had Zorro, two tables away. The assassin slipped out when Rik wasn't looking. Jen said she'd seen him heading for the trees, where the blue players were waiting, two or three hundred of them. Neither Rik nor Zorro had seen Mac since the gamekeeper introduced them. He certainly wasn't around here.

Rik texted Jen. IT'S TIME. Then he hurried to the rest rooms at the back of the café, and waited for her to arrive.

FINAL SATURDAY 1.13 P.M. – HAN

Han queued up to get her wristband in the middle of the park. She was nervous. Not because of the age thing – there was no lower age limit in the Water War game – but because of the weapons she was carrying. Like Spray, the Water War had a rule that you couldn't carry anything that resembled a real gun.

Han didn't talk to anyone else in the queue. Most of them were in gangs anyhow. She refused to make eye contact with the three men who stood on pedestals, their bodies painted white. The tall one wore swimming trunks and a turban. The fat one was in a toga, with a laurel wreath around his painted head. The small one was nearest to her height, and wore full Roman armour. For a moment, his heavily made-up eyes caught hers. She looked away. She'd seen these painted people in several places, on holiday and in the city. She always found them creepy. They might not be in the game, she figured, but they were bound to get sprayed at some point. All that white paint and make-up would end up as one hell of a mess.

It took half an hour to get to the front of the queue, but once she was there, the stewards didn't frisk her, didn't even inspect her water gun or back pack, merely took her entry fee (a small donation to charity) and stapled a cloth band to her right wrist. There was three-quarters of an hour to go before the game began: plenty of time to find her brother, who was one of the three finalists in the Spray game.

The park was a vast area of dried-up, dusty ground. The blue players – there seemed to be two or three hundred of them – were congregating on the left-hand side of the park, beyond the dry lake, near the wooded area and the bird cages.

A bloke her age began to talk to her. 'We've chosen the wrong side. There aren't many water fountains for refills round here.'

'Doesn't matter,' Han told him. 'Water here's been turned off for weeks.'

'That's right,' said one of the self-elected leaders. 'So conserve every drop you've got for spraying the enemy. If you can't spray, you can't play!'

Han wandered among the players, trying to spot her brother. If she were in the final today, she would hide herself amongst these amateurs, these day trippers of the Water War. Where was Chris?

On a small makeshift stage, the city's mayor produced a large stainless-steel whistle from the right breast pocket of his cotton shirt, stepped into the sunshine, and blew it.

The Water War was under way.

FINAL SATURDAY 2.07 P.M. – SHELL

Shell and Maiko fought side by side, charging across the park towards the red team. As soon as they were all within range of each other, water flowed freely in both directions. Both Shell and Maiko got splashed, but not sprayed directly. It was chaotic. Soon, half the players they passed were out of the game. It didn't matter what colour your wristband was. Red or blue, once it had been sprayed, the band turned purple. But players kept spraying until they were out of water, then went off in search of more.

Shell used her super-soaker with care. She wanted to last longer in this game than she had done in the Spray game. Maiko, more exuberant, was soon both eliminated and out of water. She didn't care. The two of them rested by a tree.

'Have you seen Joe?' Shell asked Maiko.

'No. Think he's with Mac?'

'Dunno. But look over there.'

Walking towards them, super-soaker in hand, was Zorro. The long-haired man wore a red wristband, like them. He and Mac were on opposite sides.

'I'm going to phone Mac,' Shell told Maiko. 'You distract Zorro.'

'How?' Maiko asked.

'Remind him that you were his first kill. Offer to team up with him or something. Go now!'

Shell got out her phone and punched in Mac's number on speed dial. She watched as Maiko joined Zorro, only for a posse of blue players to charge over the hill, and spray the couple from head to toe.

FINAL SATURDAY 2.13 P.M. – HAN

The whole thing was a farce. Red players sprayed blue players and vice versa, but team members also sprayed each other for the fun of it. Han made sure that she got sprayed early on. She didn't want to be a target, she wanted to be an onlooker. People kept spraying, even when their wristband had turned purple. The only thing that stopped people spraying was running out of water. Several had bulky reserve packs on their backs, feeding water directly into their super-soakers. They could go on for hours.

Han was constantly aware of the revolver, pressing against her ribcage. She hadn't decided whether to use it. If she did, there was no chance she'd get away with it. If the police didn't catch her, Mum would know. But there was more than one way to get revenge. Maybe Han could threaten Chris into giving up half of his inheritance. No, all of it. At one time, she would have shared, but Chris had had his chance to share and not taken it. He'd acted like he had no sister, taking everything for himself.

After today, Han realized, she might not have a brother.

At last, Han spotted someone she knew. The guy she saw was driving Mac's car the day that Han sprayed DC. He was on her brother's team. His wristband was blue, so he was still

in the water war. It was unlikely that he would lead Han to
Chris, but she decided to follow him anyway.

FINAL SATURDAY 2.17 P.M. – RIK

Rik was hot and uncomfortable, but he had a good vantage point, and to move from his position would risk exposure. Everybody in the park looked as hot as him. The day was muggy, with low cloud. All around the café and shops area, families were watching the players as they endlessly sprayed each other. Once the action slowed down, the crowd applauded every time somebody got soaked. They were probably wishing that somebody would aim a water pistol at them as well.

There were other distractions. Clowns walked by, advertising the circus which began that evening. A bouncy castle had been erected on the dry lake. Someone threw a water balloon in Rik's direction and he flinched, but it landed on the smallest of the living statues, the one in Roman armour, who swatted it aside like a fly, then let the water trickle down the gold paint of his breast plate.

Rik saw somebody he recognized. It was Zorro, accompanied by the girl whose room Rik had visited before the game began, Maiko. Zorro's side was wet, as if he'd just been sprayed. His wristband was purple. What were those two doing together?

Was this Rik's best chance of spraying the champion?

That depended on the location of Mac. To spray Zorro would be to give himself away. Rik decided that he would only spray Zorro if he was spotted. So far, his hiding place was holding up. Rik should be safe as long as he stayed still. But that was hard enough to do in this heat, with the sweat gathering and trickling down his back. Not long now, he told himself. Soon, one way or another, it would be over.

FINAL SATURDAY 2.21 P.M. – MAC

The couple were in a crowd but Zorro was easy to pick out. He was walking next to Maiko, who was taller than him. Both had been sprayed, which was sensible on Zorro's part. Players with a purple wristband blended in with the crowd. Mac was too proud a player to get sprayed. He and Joe had cut a swathe through the blue team, and their wristbands were still bright red. Shell, on the other side, still had her blue wristband. Mac hoped he didn't have to spray her. She was following Maiko and Zorro, keeping Mac informed of their every move. At the moment, they were in a crowd heading towards the café. Each was hoping to refill their pistols with water – from the tap if it was working, or, failing that, from a water bottle, if there were any left to buy. Most likely Zorro's backpack remained well stocked, but it was impossible to tell.

'This is it!' Joe told Mac. 'You duck behind that tree. I'll steer them your way!'

Mac did as they'd agreed. It was a pincer movement. Joe jumped in front of Zorro and Maiko. The crowd moved around them, separating the assassin from the bystanders. Zorro spoke.

'We're already out of the game, man. No point in spraying us.'

'Pity,' Joe said. 'But that was never my plan. Look behind you.'

Zorro tried to run. Neither Joe nor Maiko stopped him. You weren't allowed assists in the final shoot-out. Anyway, the champion was trapped. Mac's double-helix super-soaker was fully primed, and fired a wide spray. The range wasn't as good as some CPS systems, but it was good enough to get Zorro. Soon, the champion was soaked through. He laughed as Mac sprayed him, a good sport to the end.

When Mac was done, the champion bowed to Mac and handed over his laminate.

'You're one hell of a player, my friend. Congratulations. But you still have to beat Rik. Good luck with that.'

FINAL SATURDAY 2.26 P.M.
– SHELL

Shell charged through the gawping tourists and retired players, trying to spot any wristbands that were still intact. She was meant to be looking for Rik, too, but he had been invisible since the game began, nearly half an hour ago. She did notice the girl who had sprayed DC, Han. She'd read how Han had been eliminated from the game yesterday, but not who had sprayed her. It was still a big achievement, fifth place. She must congratulate her.

There was Zorro, walking away from Mac and Joe, a third-place loser. An ugly thought crossed Shell's mind. An ugly but necessary thought. Why couldn't she be a winner too? Why was it that in wars, men did all the fighting and women helped on the sidelines: cooks, camp followers, drivers, decoys? What was in this for her? A boyfriend? There was more to life than that. Shell didn't need a guy like Mac or Joe to pick her. Why was it men got to do the asking? She wanted to be a winner. She wanted to be the one who chose.

Mac and Joe's wristbands were still blue. Shell was close enough now to spray either of them. She would go for both. OK, she might only get one before she was eliminated herself. Which to choose? While she was making up her mind, it was made up for her.

'Before we go any further,' Joe said, 'I have to do this.'

Mac stood there and took it. Joe pointed his pistol. He shot at the wrist only. Mac's red wristband turned purple.

'Think you're the last player left?' Mac asked Joe.

Joe shrugged, giving the goofy grin that Shell once found endearing. Shell stepped forward and, as she did so, Maiko gasped out a warning. Maiko was only a couple of paces away from her boyfriend. She tried to throw herself in front of him. But Shell was too quick. She sprayed Joe from top to bottom, soaking his wristband in the process. Joe shook himself down before speaking to her.

'Shell, Shell. First you wouldn't go out with me, then you spray me as well. Talk about adding insult to injury. But, look out!'

She looked around. Behind Shell was Han. Up close, the girl did appear young. Fifteen probably. She reached into a holster hitherto concealed beneath her right arm. The water pistol that came out was old school. It looked like a real revolver. Shell pointed her super-soaker back at her. She still had a little water left in it. But then she noticed that Han's wristband was already purple. And she wasn't pointing the gun at Shell. She was pointing it at Mac. Didn't Han know that she was out of the Spray game?

'Is that a real gun?' Joe asked. In reply, Han aimed at Mac's head.

'You're going to pay,' she said. 'Not for the money, but for leaving me behind.'

'What is this?' Mac said. 'I've been waiting to meet you, Han. Feel free to spray me, but it won't count.'

One moment, Han's finger was on the trigger. The next, she let the gun drop.

'You're not him,' Han said.

'I'm not who?' Mac replied.

'You look like him, from a distance. But you're not Chris. You're not my brother.'

'Your brother?' Mac said. 'What's all this about?'

'I thought you were my brother, Chris, but you're not even the right nationality.' Han swore.

'He's not Chris,' said a new voice. 'I am.'

The gamekeeper stepped out of the trees. He did look like Mac. They had the same build and his hair was similar, but Mac was fairer, more conventionally good-looking. The gamekeeper had what you might call an interesting face, rather than a handsome one. His jaw was a little pointed. His eyes were deep set, and, close up, they had a haunted look about them. Shell couldn't take her eyes off him.

'Hi, sis,' the gamekeeper said. 'Sorry it's been so long. I was going to call you when this game was over, I swear.'

The young girl lifted the gun and, for a moment, Shell thought that she would point it again. Her hands were shaking, but she put it back in the holster. When she'd done this, Han burst into tears. Her brother stepped forward and embraced her. Suddenly, lots of people were approaching. Shell thought that they were looking at Han, or Mac, or the gamekeeper. But they weren't. They were looking at her.

'She's the one!' Shell heard someone say.

'Hold up your arm!' one of the stewards ordered, and she did.

'Her band's still red! She's the one!' the steward announced. 'We have a winner!'

FINAL SATURDAY 2.41 P.M. – MAC

The centre of the park was so crowded that Rik could be anywhere. The day had turned muggy and overcast. In the gloom, it was hard to spot faces in the crowd. But Rik was a big guy. Mac would find him first, as long as he avoided places the assassin could hide behind.

Mac had Joe to one side of him and Maiko on the other. Shell had been escorted away to be feted as the winner of the Water War. Mac was proud of her, of course he was, but what she had won paled into insignificance compared to what he was on the verge of achieving. Any minute now, he could be champion at the third attempt. He had already taken out Zorro. Once he got Rik, Mac would feel like the king of the world. Mac loved this game. He could play it for the rest of his life. There was a loud rumbling noise nearby.

'I hate to tell you this,' Joe said, 'but I think it's going to . . .'

The first drops of rain began to fall, removing the need for Joe to finish the sentence. The thunder cracked loudly, just the other side of the lake. From all over the park, people began to run towards the shop and café, looking for cover.

'First rain in weeks and weeks,' Maiko said. 'Couldn't it have waited a few more minutes?'

The rain poured, smashing on to the dry, cracked ground.

'Think we should find some cover?' Joe asked Mac.

'I don't mind being wet,' Mac told him. 'It's kind of refreshing, don't you think? Mind you, I wouldn't want to be them!'

He pointed at the three living statues, who were still standing on their plinths, watching the crowd run for shelter. The white paint was pouring from their bodies, revealing pale skin beneath. The small one in armour got off his plinth first, holding his shield over his head to act as an umbrella. Then the tall one stepped down from his pedestal. Only then did Mac take a good look at the fat one in the middle. He wore a toga and had a laurel wreath around his head. He looked kind of familiar. The statue reached into his toga and pulled out a tiny red water pistol.

'Sorry, dude,' Rik said, as he pointed the pistol. Before Mac had time to react, the white statue fired the water pistol and landed a direct shot on Mac's head. The game was over.

THIRD SUNDAY 8.46 P.M. – MAC

The party was warming up. Chris took Mac to one side.

'I should have won,' Mac said. 'I was so near, I could taste it.'

'It's not about the winning,' the gamekeeper told Mac. 'It's about how you play. You've got lots of money. You could have done the game the easy way, like Badmonkey, and used hired help. But no, you took the hard way, persuaded people to help you make it to the last two. Respect.'

'I plan to enter again, win next time,' Mac insisted.

'That might be harder than you think,' Chris told him. 'Zorro's retiring and Rik says he's not interested in defending his championship, so you'd be the player to beat. It's a lot harder to win when you're not just another anonymous player.'

Behind them, nearly all of the game's two hundred entrants had arrived at the student centre. Only one notable player was missing.

'So Han's your sister,' Mac said to Chris. 'What happened there?'

'Nasty divorce,' Chris said. 'My mum left my dad for another bloke. As soon as I turned sixteen, a couple of months later, I chose to live with my dad. My sister stayed with Mum and her new bloke, who was a creep. Dad was a workaholic, built up an even bigger business after Mum left him. He worked himself to death in eighteen months. And he left me everything. I'm rich. Whereas Mum's second husband spent all of the money she'd got off Dad then dumped her. Not that Han and Mum are poor, exactly. Dad left a trust fund to pay for Han's education.

'I shouldn't have lost touch with her, or taken all the money. But I was hurt, and angry. In a divorce, people take sides, like it's some kind of game. Now I need to build bridges with her and Mum. I'm just hoping she shows up tonight. But that's enough about me. What about you? What will you do next?'

Mac shrugged. 'No idea. Any suggestions?'

Chris leant closer to him. 'I do have one idea. I've been the gamekeeper for two years, since I won the game in Seattle. Playing the game, then running the game got me through some rough times after Dad died. But I'm through. I've decided to go to university here, get to know my family again. That means I need somebody to take over from me, someone who loves the game, and can afford to devote a lot of time to it. Somebody like you. Interested?'

'I'm tempted,' Mac said.

'No hurry,' Chris said. 'Whatever you decide, it'll be our secret. Tell me after I've made the presentation. But I really hope you'll do it. I can't think of anyone better, and I hate not to get my way.'

He vanished into the throng. Mac looked around the party. He recognized a lot of the guests, and they were good people. There was The Invisible Man, dancing with DC. A

TV game show host was talking to Jal, the schoolteacher. The bald guy who'd been his first assassin was chatting up a smart, professional-looking woman. Jen was tucked under Rik's left arm. Joe was kissing Maiko. Shell was in the middle of the dance floor, wearing her Water War winner's medal. As Mac watched, Chris joined her and began to dance.

Behind Shell was a nurse, whose boyfriend, the policeman, was talking to an old guy in a wheelchair. Zorro was surrounded by well-wishers, but, sensing Mac's stare, he looked up, twirled his moustache and gave Mac a friendly wave. At the entrance, Mac saw Han arrive. With her hair down and her mask gone, she looked terrific. How old was she? Fifteen and a half. Only two years younger than him. Han walked tentatively into the room, looking for someone. Mac knew who that was. He walked over to the gamekeeper, nodded at Shell, then pointed out the new guest to Chris.

'By the way, I don't need time to decide,' Mac added, speaking softly into Chris's ear. 'My mind's made up. I'll do it. I'll take your place.'

THIRD SUNDAY 8.55 P.M. – HAN

Han still had the gun. In the confusion when she mistook Mac for Chris, nobody had made sure that what she was carrying was only a water pistol. The revolver was in the concealed holster beneath her right shoulder, ready for her to pull out when the moment was right.

It was nearly time for the prize giving. Han moved across the crowded dance floor, looking for Chris. Then she spotted him. He was next to Mac, her erstwhile target. Chris was dancing with the girl who won the Water War, a gorgeous blonde in a white linen dress. More competition for her brother's attention. Then Han remembered that Shell, while she might have been eliminated, almost succeeded in spraying her early on. She was a worthy competitor.

Mac finished speaking to Chris and at last her brother turned round, noticed her. He hurried over, pushing through the crowd.

'Han!' Chris began to speak in a rush. The music was loud and Han couldn't make out all the words. He was apologizing for losing touch, for hiding from them. It was sickening. Han could shoot him here and now. But she knew she wouldn't. Chris leant closer.

'I should have known you'd join the game. I'm sorry. I

blocked you out of my life for three years. I tried to pretend you didn't exist.'

'I missed Dad's funeral,' Han said, making herself angry to keep back from crying. The revolver seemed to throb against her arm. Chris tried to hug her, but she pushed him back. She didn't want him to feel the gun. 'How could you let me miss saying goodbye?'

'I was selfish and stupid and angry,' he said. 'About the money,' he added. 'I'll make it all right. Half of it should be yours.'

'I never cared about the money,' she told him. 'I cared about you. And Spray. I'll be sixteen in seven months. Where's the game going next? No way are you going to stop me winning next time.'

Before her brother could reply, the music stopped. The DJ spoke.

'Players, make way for your new champion!'

With a great cheer, the dancers pushed back, creating a corridor for Rik. The winner hugged his girlfriend, gave a bashful smile, then strode forward to collect his prize. All but two of the players raised their water pistols to the ceiling. Then they turned their super-soakers to the new champion.

'This bit's traditional,' Chris told Han, as Rik got the good soaking he had avoided until now.

Han turned to look at the one other player who wasn't holding a water pistol. Mac. They had unfinished business.

She winked at him. He blew her a kiss.

'Next year,' she mouthed, then blew him a kiss back.